"Are you ha̶̶̶̶̶̶̶ at this...singles̶ night?

"Me? No-ho-ho. I mean, sure. Meeting people is always nice, don't you think?"

Dante did not.

She held out both hands, closed her eyes, then looked him in the eye. "Short answer—*life's* short. So what do you say? Wanna help us do this thing?"

He wanted to shut down anything involving this woman being anywhere near him. But he was there to wrestle the Vine and Stein into the black. And Sutton had just offered up a big step toward doing that.

As if she could sense his defenses melting, she smiled and said, *"Bene?"*

"Sì. Bene."

Sutton clapped her hands and jumped up and down. Then, before he felt her move, she took a large step and threw her arms around his neck. As if time slowed, he could feel the warmth of her through her thin T-shirt, and a soft puff of her breath kissed his ear.

Sparks went off behind his eyes, his body reacting to the feel of her, her warm scent, her life force, in more ways than he could counter.

Dear Reader,

A few months ago, I had an idea for a story set in a South Australian winery. I like wine, but I'm a true novice, so a research trip was surely in order.

I called my wonderful friend—author and foodie Clare Connelly—and said, "If I came your way, might you have time to join me at a winery for some research?"

Cue a full-on girls' trip, with Amy Andrews coming along for the fun, covering multiple wine regions, over three days, and three times as many cellar door tastings, with sommeliers looking at us in panic as I whipped out my trusty notebook and pen, promising all characters would be fictional to protect the innocent.

The scenery was spectacular, the company unparalleled, the wines truly delicious, and the knowledge imparted by so many generous people was more than I could have hoped for.

Any errors in vineyard lore are my own!

I hope you love the delightful town of Vermillion, and the stories held in its warm embrace, for this story is a heartfelt ode to friendship, to that trip, small-town Australia and the people we meet along the way.

Love,

Ally

xxx

DATING DEAL WITH THE ITALIAN

ALLY BLAKE

ROMANCE

Harlequin®
ROMANCE

ISBN-13: 978-1-335-21635-9

Dating Deal with the Italian

Harlequin Enterprises ULC
22 Adelaide St. West, 41st Floor
Toronto, Ontario M5H 4E3, Canada
www.Harlequin.com

Printed in U.S.A.

Recycling programs for this product may not exist in your area.

Australian author **Ally Blake** loves reading and strong coffee, porch swings and dappled sunshine, beautiful notebooks and soft, dark pencils. Her inquisitive, rambunctious, spectacular children are her exquisite delights. And she adores writing love stories so much she'd write them even if nobody else read them. No wonder, then, having sold over four million copies of her romance novels worldwide, Ally is living her bliss. Find out more about Ally's books at allyblake.com.

Books by Ally Blake

Harlequin Romance

Billion-Dollar Bachelors

Whirlwind Fling to Baby Bombshell
Fake Engagement with the Billionaire
Cinderella Assistant to Boss's Bride

One Year to Wed

Secretly Married to a Prince

Hired by the Mysterious Millionaire
A Week with the Best Man
Crazy About Her Impossible Boss
Brooding Rebel to Baby Daddy
Dream Vacation, Surprise Baby
The Millionaire's Melbourne Proposal
The Wedding Favor
Always the Bridesmaid

Visit the Author Profile page
at Harlequin.com for more titles.

This book is dedicated to "great legs,"
"blame the fingerprints," "smells like grape" and the
#winerywednesday crowd. You know who you are.

Praise for
Ally Blake

CHAPTER ONE

SUTTON MAYBERRY BOPPED along with the demo album of an indie band she was considering managing as she drove along the gently curving country road.

She smiled as she tipped her face to the sunshine dappling the windscreen of her rental car. Yet, when the GPS informed her that she would soon be turning left in order to "reach her destination," for the briefest of moments she considered driving on.

Which was silly. It had been her choice to hop on a plane and fly halfway across the world on a whim, and she was willing, nay, delighted to be there.

As if deciding to gift Sutton one more layer of delight, the forest she'd been driving through cleared, giving way to a view that had her blinking in enchantment. Pretty green paddocks dotted with fluffy white sheep nestled up against small, neat farmhouses boasting windmills and water tanks, and hillside after hillside covered in striations of fantastically twisted grape vines.

When instructed she did take that left, and found herself driving beneath a large, arched, wooden sign reading Welcome to Vermillion: You Are Entering Wine Country.

The Main Street of Vermillion was straight out of a rom-com. Shop fronts with pretty striped awnings, cottage gardens bursting with roses bordered in old stone fences covered in moss, picture windows glowing with golden inner lights. Handmade signs boasted local cheeses, cosy cafés, vintage clothes, bric-a-brac, homegrown vegetables, and baskets of grain ready for milling.

And if the "welcome" sign hadn't made it clear she'd entered "wine country," the grape carvings on every shop sign, and the grape vines curling around lampposts and drooping elegantly from pergola rooves, sure did the trick.

Sutton slowed to a stop at a pedestrian crossing as a pair of old ladies crossed the road, nattering happily, arms intertwined. She took the chance to let the window down and breathe deep of the soft spring air. It smelled sweet, floral and crisp. A million miles from the drizzle, and crowds, and hustle, and sticky pub floors, and loud music she'd left behind in central London a little over twenty-four hours before.

She smiled at the apologetic mother of a young toddler who'd started across the road, then stopped to pick up treasures along the way. Then her heart felt a little yank. Rewind time and that curious, curly-haired toddler might have been her.

For it was here, in this grape-laden hamlet, that her parents had first met. Fallen in love at first sight, no less. Her father been a backpacker, working behind the bar in a local pub, when the door opened, "bringing with it a shaft of sunlight, and within the beam the most beautiful woman he'd ever seen."

She could hear her father's voice; the storied tale of high romance having been narrated to her so many times over the years she could recite it by rote.

It had ended tragically, her mother dying when only a few weeks older than Sutton was now. Heartbroken, her darling father had whisked their small family back to London, turning Vermillion into a fairy-tale land in her mind, rather than a real place.

Until now.

A car behind her beeped. With a wave out the window, Sutton rolled the car through the empty crossing and looked for a place to park.

Before she found a place to stay, she wanted to check in with her bands, let them know she'd arrived safe and sound. And her dad? *Not yet*, she thought, a frisson of guilt skittering up the back of her neck.

For all that he talked so fondly of Vermillion, it was inextricably tied up in the loss of her mother, whom he mourned, to that day. She didn't want to do anything to exacerbate that. So, she'd let him imagine her in Amsterdam with the Magnolia Blossoms, or Belgium with the Sweety Pies—he loved to keep track of where her bands were playing, even if his taste went more to Bowie than it did to modern punk, or jazz-funk.

He'd be thrilled she'd finally made the pilgrimage; she was *sure* of it. She'd just wait to let him know once she had something to share.

Now, having forgotten to grab an Australian sim card at the airport, finding a place with free Wi-Fi was key. And…there! A spot.

She pulled into the angled park, then looked up to find herself outside a yarn store. The sign read Swirl & Purl Craft Corner. On the left of it was a small old-timey cinema—the Hollywood and Vine—boasting a twilight showing of *Calamity Jane*. On the right was a gift shop called Wine Not?

Sutton huffed out a laugh. While her tastes ran more to indie horror, black jeans and T-shirts, and dark craft beer, she could see how her dad would have found such pleasure in this place.

Grabbing her slouchy black leather backpack from the passenger seat, she hopped out of the car, twisted back and forth a little to stretch out the kinks, then looked up the street.

Her gaze landed on a classic pub sign hanging from a horizontal pole high up on the outer wall of a big black brick building a few doors up. *Excellent*, she thought as she strode up the path. She'd grab a coffee, a bite to eat, and the Wi-Fi password, find a place to stay, and fend off jet lag as long as she could.

Rather imposing, the place was, up close and personal. Especially when compared with the twee architecture on the rest of the street. Tall, old brick, the facade painted matte black, bar the double-story windows along half the wall.

The sign above the door read Vine and Stein. She wondered if the inhabitants of the town were simply all delightful, pun-loving people, or if some town provenance made it compulsory.

Then, reaching to push open the door, she stopped at the last when some wave of energy, like déjà vu only stronger, swept over her. Her hand whipped back to hold the strap of her bag.

What if this was the pub in which her parents had first met? She flicked through her memories, but couldn't say if father had mentioned the *name* of the place, preferring to focus on the fairy tale, high points of falling in love.

She could message her dad and ask, but that would mean telling him where she was.

That could all come later, once she'd found her feet in the town in which she was born, a few weeks off the same age her mother had been when she'd died.

She'd lived with a ticking clock in the back of

her head her entire life, born of the knowledge that it could all be taken without warning. It had been the impetus to throw herself at any opportunity that came her way.

No point holding back now, she thought.

Then she reached out and opened the door.

Dante Rossi had come to the conclusion that choosing to curse in Italian or English made no difference when attempting to feel less aggrieved about doing something he did not wish to do.

Far too big to be wedged beneath the Vine and Stein bar, shoulder on the verge of popping from its socket as he attempted to unscrew the bolt welding the vintage cash register to the bench above, that realisation came far too late.

I missed harvest for this, he thought, wrenching with all his might. Without result.

Autumn festivals, popular throughout Umbria, and the resultant uptick in vineyard tours, the influx of people in general, he could miss. But that handful of days when the delicate balance between allowing a crop to ripen to perfection and deciding the exact right moment to reap—that was pure magic.

"Al diavolo tutto," Dante swore through gritted teeth, cursing this place, this town, and his agreement to have anything to do with either of them when he ought to be back home, answering only to his own conscience.

"Ah, hello?"

Dante flinched at the unexpected voice, knocking his elbow against the underside of the bar. As numbing sparks shot up his arm, he let his eyes drift closed and imagined the hum of bees, the twitter of small birds the only sound for miles—

"Hello, down there?" the voice called again.

Dante twisted his head out from under the bar so that he might glance toward the office, and shout, "Chrissy! *Sei qui?*" in the hopes the day manager, who had disappeared some time ago, had returned.

"Back in a tick!" Chrissy had said the moment he had arrived. Dante had assumed "a tick" meant a short amount of time. Clearly it was yet one more Australianism he did not understand, as silence, bar the staticky, electric hum of the refrigeration system, gave him his answer.

He heard the scrape of a shoe and stilled. "Chrissy?"

"Nope!" said the dismembered voice, cheerfully. "I'm Sutton. Are you okay down there? Do you need some help?"

Dante did not need help. Not the kind the voice was suggesting, anyway.

Rewind a month, to when Zia Celia had called, begging him to come to Vermillion, to save the family vineyard—that was when *help* might have been of use. Some voice that reminded him why he stayed on his own estate and left the world to its own devices.

"Look, I think I should come back there—?"

"No," he growled. *"Il bar è chiuso.* The bar is closed."

Back home—what with siestas and long lunches and time at the vineyard linked more to sunshine and seasons than to clocks—it would not occur to him to give a damn. But here, every misstep added interminable additional time to his burden.

Using his rising ire, Dante white-knuckled the arm of the wrench, and pulled. His arms shook with exertion, the muscles between his shoulders screamed. He could do this; whatever it took to rid himself of any last vestiges of the remorse his aunt had used to get him there, and then he could go home.

"Are you sure?" asked the voice. "The sign on the door says 'open.' And when I gave the door a push, I was clearly able to enter."

Dante let the wrench fall to the floor with a clang, then lay back, breathing hard, and came as close to laughing as he had done in weeks. A laugh built on frustration—with this place, and with himself.

A bead of sweat trickled down his neck and he wondered when he might get time to shower, rid himself of whatever filth he was lying in. Hell, maybe he'd shave his head and burn all his clothes.

But first… He considered his nemesis. Not Australian. English? Female, most definitely. Obstinate, or wilfully obtuse.

"Note," he said, slowing his cadence, "the chairs atop the tables. The fact we are on emergency lights only. And if you look around you will see no other people in here bar yourself. I suggest those points back up my assertion."

When he heard nothing more from the other side of the bar, he assumed the intruder had moved on. He wondered if he might allow himself to take that as having managed to achieve one thing that day.

At the clearing of a nearby throat, Dante sent a short, sharp, tempestuous message to the gods, then heaved himself out from under the bar, enough to have a partial view of the owner of the voice leaning over it.

Dark silhouette, sunglasses atop long dark hair, backlit by the weak sunlight pouring through the street-side windows.

His choices came down to a) insisting the woman leave, b) ignoring her if she did not, or c) as his cousin Niccolo liked to say, *act like a human person* and help her with whatever it was that had sent her into the place, and *then* move her on, so he could get this one damn thing done right.

He gripped the edge of the bar and used it to leverage himself out from under the cabinetry.

Sitting up, he wiped his hands on the knees of his jeans, tugged at the shirt stuck to him in several places—with sweat or old beer—then uncurled himself to standing.

"What is so important that—" Dante stopped, his next words drying up in his throat.

For the silhouette had moved with him, tipping back as he stood, revealing a face so lovely, so luminous, he could not recall what he'd been about to say. Drinking her in, he noted dark hair falling about her shoulders like ribbons, skin like sunshine on cream, cheekbones for days. Soft blue eyes, *bedroom eyes*, he thought, before he could stop himself.

Then she smiled and something pinged inside his head. Like a beacon. Or a warning.

"Wow," she said, laughing, her eyes sparking with light, "you're an absolute mess. What were you doing down there?"

He swallowed, surprised to find himself parched; like a man who had stepped out of the desert to find himself yearning not for water, but for a 1967 Leroy Musigny Grand Cru. Yet, Dante was not a man who *yearned*. His life—bar the last two weeks spent in this time-sucking, quicksand of a place— was exactly as he'd curated it to be. And far better than he deserved.

Certain he must have stood up too fast, for it was the only explanation for his discomfiture, Dante rolled his neck, ran sticky fingers through his tangled hair, then went to rest his knuckles on the bar, only to find they were covered in grease.

Crossing his arms, hands curled into fists, he looked into the woman's twinkling blue eyes and said, "What is it that you want, Ms....?"

"Mayberry," she said. "Sutton Mayberry." Smile widening as she looked around the bar, she added, "Don't you think bars and pubs feel strange when it's this quiet. It's as if this building is holding its breath, waiting for music and people to spill in through the cracks and fill the place with noise and light and grit and life."

Dante, who had seen at most a hundred people come into this white elephant of a business over the course of each day since he'd been there, felt tired imagining the scene she described.

Seeming to take his silence for agreement, the stranger lifted her sunglasses off her head to slip them into a soft leather backpack she'd dropped onto a barstool. She grabbed another barstool, sat, and said, "Well, are you going to offer me a drink?"

"A drink," he parroted, feeling warmth creep into his skin, his bones.

Elbows on the bar, she smiled up at him "This *is* a bar, right?"

"Si," he allowed. Then glanced right, to the big carriage clock on the wall between the front door and the kitchen. "It's eleven in the morning."

"Which makes it happy hour somewhere."

She was right, only it made his thoughts turn once more to home. He calculated it was around three in the morning at Sorello, the vineyard he owned and ran. All would be quiet there, bar the skitter of mice, and the groan of old wood—the comforting sounds of night in a three-hundred-year-old villa.

Brow tight, he looked back to find the intruder watching him. Long, dark lashes swept against her cheeks when she blinked, slowly, making his fingertips prickle, as if his blood was slipping and pooling in places it wasn't used to.

Needing space, he moved to the sink to scrub his hands clean. Then grabbed the hand towel and twisted it around his fingers to ground himself. He motioned to the bottles lined up in front of the mirror behind the bar, and asked, "What'll it be?"

"Are you kidding? It's eleven in the morning." A quick irreverent smile, then, "I've been on a plane for most of the past twenty-four hours, so would give anything for a coffee."

As one they looked to the machine that sat cold and still down the other end of the bar; not yet switched on for the day.

Because the Vine was closed.

When Dante did nothing to rectify the fact, the woman laughed, a soft husky sound, before saying, "How about a glass of water?"

"Still or sparkling?"

"Sparkling," she said, lifting her hands to hold

them under her chin as she sparkled with all her might.

It was dazzling. She was dazzling. But Dante was not to be dazzled. He could only hope that the flat stare he offered in return made that perfectly clear.

When she dropped her hands, her front teeth, a little longer than the rest, caught on her bottom lip with a slow drag.

And Dante… Dante needed this over and done with.

He reached for a glass from the rack above, filled it with ice, then poured her a glass of sparkling water on tap.

Habit born of weeks spent learning the ins and outs of the pub—trying to figure out why it was not pulling its weight within the Rossi portfolio of investments—had him turning to the cash register, only to remember it was broken. And heaviness pressed down on him once more.

He slid the drink in front of her. "On the house."

"Oh. Are you sure? Because—" One hand reached out to clasp the glass—short fingernails, shiny black polish—while the other tapped a finger on the bar.

"Was there something else? Perhaps you'd like me to cook you a three-course meal, wash your car, do your taxes…"

"That would be all amazing, but honestly, just your Wi-Fi password would suffice." It came with a smile that had no doubt gotten her what she wanted on any number of occasions.

Dante pointed to a laminated sign over the bar—username and password printed thereon. "If that's all?"

"It is," she promised, sliding off the barstool, grabbing her backpack, and slinging it over one shoulder. "I'll just…find a spot back there in the dark. Stay out of your way. Let you get back to…"

Tipping up onto her toes, she leaned over the bar, and waggled her fingers at the floor. When she looked back up, she was close. So close Dante felt a wash of softness, like sunshine on dust motes at the corners of his vision.

He could not have been more relieved when she gave him a nod of thanks, then made her way to a table near the farthest window, where a slab of sunlight poured into the bar. She took down the chairs, arranging them neatly, then sat on one in a slump of long limbs.

After looking out the window for a long moment, sighing, then running her hands over her face, she reached into her bag, pulled out a phone, and was soon lost to whatever it was his Wi-Fi helped her to do.

Not *his* Wi-Fi.

It was Zia Celia's. And his cousin Niccolo and cousin Aurora, who was getting up to mischief overseas. They, along with Dante's uncle Giacomo, had left Italy decades before, moving to

South Australia to run the Vermillion Hill vineyard, and much of the real estate in town along with it. At the behest of Rossi Vignaioli Internazionali. Or, more specifically, Dante's father, who back then had run it all.

This responsibility Dante currently held for this place came by way of tendrils of duty and guilt, ancient turmoil that stretched all the way from the other side of the world. And back through time.

Once he had done as his aunt had requested, and found a pathway to bring the Vine and Stein back into the black, he could leave behind the twee shops and familial pressure, and return to the scent of olive trees, and old wood, and Italian earth. He could go home.

Laughter carried across the large near-empty space, as the intruder read something that tickled her. The sound curled inside him, warm and soothing. And while he did not wish to, Dante moved to the coffee machine and switched it on.

The thing let out a loud hiss as the water began to steam, and over the top of the machine, he saw the intruder look up. Sit up. Her face filled with hope.

"How long?" she called.

"Half hour to warm up," Dante responded.

"I'm pretty sure I can survive just that long. Black, please, when you're ready. Bitter is fine. And extra hot. If you're worried it might burn the roof of my mouth, it'll be perfect."

If Dante needed one more thing to convince him the world beyond his borders was a wild and unruly place, the thought of someone searing their taste buds, deliberately, rendering them unable to fully enjoy the pleasure that was a grape weathered by the elements, delicately plucked, liquefied, fermented, curated, stored, and turned into a life-affirming drop was it.

"Heathen," he muttered, as he set a series of espresso cups atop the machine in order to warm them.

Catching sight of the sleeve of his shirt, the smear of dirt thereupon, he glanced to the mirror behind the bar. Grease smeared his cheek, his hair was tangled with sweat, his brow deeply furrowed. He looked a wreck. He felt it too. As if his very marrow was suffering.

A small spark of light in his day thus far, Dante remembered he had spare clothes in the office, stashed there in case he ever needed to sleep on the small couch, if staying with his aunt and cousins became too much.

He considered letting the customer know he'd be off the floor. Then looked to the ancient cast-iron register. If she wanted it, she was welcome to it.

Emails and DMs checked, follow-ups sent, local shop from which to grab an Australian sim card sourced, bands advised she was back on deck,

Sutton sent her dad a quick, "Have to postpone next week's lunch. Fill you in soon!"

Then dropped her phone to the table as if it might burn.

Fine. She was being a scaredy-cat. Still, better to fill her dad in once she'd seen more of Vermillion, so that she could lean into nostalgia rather than the "this was where you last saw Mum" angle. Right? Right.

Sutton reached for her espresso only to find she'd finished it.

The grumpy barman had—grudgingly—done a bang-up job of giving her exactly what she'd asked for. *Hot and deliciously bitter.* The coffee, that was, not the grumpy barman. Though as descriptors went...

She looked up, hoping to catch a glimpse of him hunched over the bar, mumbling becomingly. Alas he was nowhere to be seen.

Big, he was, and tall, and broad with it. All dark eyes, tortured brow, scruffy stubble and thick wavy hair that fell over his face; a gruff, swarthy kind of hot. Add that deep, Italian drawl—a velvet rumble any singer would kill for—and the tragic air of a wintry moor, a crumbling castle, a fallen angel, when he'd hauled himself up from beneath the bar it had been a *moment*.

Eyes unfocused, as she looked into the middle distance, Sutton felt the yawn coming before she could stop it. If she stayed put in the sunshiny window, she'd likely fall asleep where she sat.

Gathering her things, she made her way through the labyrinth of tables. The chairs had all been taken down by then, a handful of patrons had come in, the scent of lunch was on the air. Other staff now loitered behind the bar—a woman with a vibrant blue pixie cut absently dried glasses, a guy with a man bun appeared to struggle with the cash register drawer.

And while she felt a flicker of disappointment that she'd not get one final glance at the hot, bitter barman, Sutton wasn't in Vermillion looking for *that*. *Was she?* No.

The strange crackle she'd felt in the air when their eyes had met had to be down to the fact she'd walked into the place thinking about her parents, and how *they'd* met. Nothing more.

When Man Bun looked up, she waved and called out her thanks, then headed back out into the soft South Australian sunshine happy to put the Vine and Stein behind her.

Sutton walked the length of Main Street, passing a thrift shop, Corker of a Deal; a menswear store, Vine and Dandy; and noting other eateries in which she might be able to sit for a bit and work each day.

Living out of her suitcase, following her bands around the world for most of her adult life, she was used to renting tables in cafés for the price of coffee and a bite to eat. No point getting used to a home office when she'd never settled into any place long enough to call it "home."

She was looking at the menu of massages and facials on a sign outside the Wine Down Day Spa, wondering if it had existed when her parents had lived there, when someone cleared their throat.

A blonde woman in a fitted red dress and red stilettos, a pastry half hanging out of her mouth, arms filled with books, gave her a deadpan stare, and Sutton realised she was blocking the footpath.

"So sorry!" said Sutton with a self-deprecating laugh, as she hustled out of the way. "Daydreaming."

The woman tugged the pastry from her mouth and said, "Best way to spend one's time." Then her book pile began to slip.

Sutton leaped forward and grabbed the top book. Then the next few as well.

The woman popped the pastry back between her teeth, then tipped her head sideways toward the building next door—a darling, whitewashed wood cottage with black shutters and window planters overflowing with colourful pansies.

It was adorable. Until one stepped inside, and things took a turn. The walls were still a bright white but everything else—lush velvet couches, huge fluffy cushions, gilt-framed art—was a riot of bright pink, blood orange, and deep aquamarine.

All of which was in service of tightly packed rows of floor-to-ceiling bookshelves chock-full of books, the covers of which woke Sutton faster than an espresso ever could. For there were half-clad Vikings, swoony cartoony rom-coms, beefy highlanders in short kilts, long-haired, muscular, lusty-looking men with wings, or fangs, or both.

"Feel as if you've stepped through a portal," the woman asked, reading Sutton's mind, "leaving behind the wholesome dreamscape that is Vermillion?"

"A little bit," Sutton admitted, looking at one of the books she'd carried in to find what appeared to be a naked space cowboy on the cover. "What is this place?"

"A haven for women who love fairies and dragons and dream of the men who morph into them. I'm Laila. Book pusher. Pleasure enabler."

"Sutton Mayberry," said Sutton. "Manager of indie bands. Pleasure enjoyer."

Giving Sutton's black leather jacket over black jeans over black Vans a once-over, Laila said, "I'm guessing you're not from around here."

"Well, I kind of am, actually," said Sutton. "My parents met here, in Vermillion. Fell in love, had me. Though we moved away when I was a toddler and I've not been back since."

Laila leaned her hip against the sales desk. "Vermillion is the setting of your origin story."

"I guess it is," Sutton said, quite liking how that sounded.

"Flying visit, or sticking around?" Laila asked as she flipped out a small stepladder, then clicked at Sutton to hand her the books she'd carried inside so she could place them on a shelf behind the counter. Tucked in between two rather spicy-looking bookends.

"Staying," Sutton said. "For a little while, at least." She wasn't sure how long, or what she hoped to find there, or much really, bar the fact she'd had to come.

"Here with anyone?" Laila asked, as she bobbed her way back down the ladder.

"Nope. I'm all alone." Sutton laughed at herself. "And that sounded more forlorn than I meant it to."

"Would you like it to be otherwise?" Laila asked, an eyebrow lifting suggestively.

Oh, thought Sutton, not having picked up that kind of vibe. "That's terribly sweet, but I'm straight, sorry."

Laila's eyes widened before she burst into laughter. "As am I, honey. As am I."

Sutton slapped a hand over her eyes in mortification. First the thing with the grumpy bartender—she was certain now that she'd stared at the veins roping up his sizeable forearms when he'd crossed his arms at her, and sighed, out loud, when he'd shaken his hair off his face only for it to fall instantly back over his brow in a Byronic sweep. Then assuming Laila had hit on her?

The "my parents met and fell in love here" thing was clearly doing a number on her!

"I'm so sorry," she said. "You found me out there, attempting to walk off jet lag before finding somewhere to stay. My people skills are clearly halfway between here and London."

"It's all good," said Laila, waving a hand over her face. "What about him—he your type?"

Sutton flinched. Then blinked to find Laila motioning to the book cover she'd rested her other hand on—a woman was entwined, intimately, with what appeared to be some kind of half man, half octopus.

Sutton curled her fingers into her palm. "My taste tends toward humans."

Laila laughed. "I was talking fiction, not real life. But since you brought it up—what's your jam? Brunettes? Blonds? Beefcake? Mamma's boys?"

When Sutton opened her mouth, then closed it again, unsure as to how the conversation had turned that way, Laila grinned.

"When I found you on the street you weren't the only one daydreaming. I was tinkering with an idea I've been playing with for some time—a fun way for young single locals to meet up." She pointed to herself. "And there you were, *all alone*, like some sign from the universe."

Octopus men, maybe not. But timing, connection, kismet—Sutton was fine with all of that. In fact, most of her greatest adventures were due to following breadcrumbs the universe had set down. All the while, the ticking clock in the back of her head, urging her on.

Laila held up both hands and moved around behind the sales desk. "Let's start fresh. You said you were looking for a place to stay?"

"I'll find something," Sutton assured her. While going with the flow wasn't for everyone—give her the day and time and she could tell you exactly what her dad would be doing—it was her normal.

"How about I'll do you a deal," said Laila. "I can hook you up with a room in a really sweet place, if you meet for me brunch tomorrow. Be my sounding board for the idea I was toying with when I banged into you."

Sutton opened her mouth to say she could sort herself out, but a yawn came out instead. "I might have to take you up on that."

Laila grabbed a notepad and scribbled something down using a pen with a fluffy pom-pom atop. "I know Barry, the owner of a local B&B. Between us, I'm his secret supply of Minotaur romances, so he'll never do me wrong."

Sutton looked to the notepaper. "The Grape Escape?"

Laila's lip curled. "I know. It's an epidemic."

Sutton looked around. "What have you called this place?"

Laila, phone now to her ear, smiled irreverently. "Well, has that been an adventure. I believe I've chosen the perfect name—with a wink to wine, which the local establishment all but insists on—but they do not agree."

"The local establishment?"

"This town is run by a single family. I've been here three months now and their *representative* has popped in at least twice a week since, ostensibly to check if I am a happy little renter, while offering alternatives such as Pages and Pinot. Romance and Riesling." She rolled her eyes at both.

"As opposed to…"

Laila held up a finger. "Barry!" she said into the phone. "It's Laila from Forbidden Fruits."

Sutton laughed. Yeah, she could see how the Swirl & Purl Craft Corner crowd might not be au fait with that one. Less than half a day and this place was already turning out to be all kinds of fun.

When a minute later, Sutton was assured she had a room as long as she needed it, she wondered if she should buy something, to pay Laila back for the favour. Slightly terrified she might then read something she could never unsee, she said, "How does late lunch sound, in case I sleep through brunch? My treat."

"That'll work."

Picturing the bakery with the great-looking meat pies, the lovely café with the mouthwatering pastries, Sutton found herself saying, "I had pretty great coffee just now, at the pub up the road. The Vine and Stein?"

Something flashed across Laila's eyes before she said, "Sure. Why not?"

"Okay." Then, as she reached the door, Sutton turned back. "Laila?"

Laila, who had already opened a book with a man covered in green fur on the cover and started reading, looked up. "Hmm?"

"Have a list of alternative names at the ready, for when the 'establishment' next comes around."

"Such as?"

Sutton, who'd had a lot of experience helping her clients settle on band names over the years, had a quick think and suggested, "Kink and Cabernet?"

Laila barked out a laugh, then, eyes twinkling, grabbed pen and paper, writing madly as Sutton went out the door.

A half hour later, Sutton dragged her suitcase into the attic room of the Grape Escape.

"This suffice?" asked Barry, thin moustache twitching, as if the fact she was an acquaintance of Laila's meant she might take off with his candlesticks.

The roof was so slanted she had to duck. The

bedspread was covered in big pink cabbage roses. The wallpaper was so fussy it made her feel a little dizzy. And she'd probably not have noticed the Minotaur lamp if not for Laila's inside info.

"It's perfect," she assured him. "Truly. I'm all appreciation."

Barry blushed red. Then, bowing slightly, backed away. "Breakfast is six till eight every day, bar Tuesdays. Fresh towels and bedding twice a week. We can organise any number of winery tours at reception."

"I'm not really a wine drinker, but thank you."

At that, Barry's eyebrows disappeared into his hairline.

Then he left her to fall face down on the softest bed that ever existed.

A minute later, after marvelling that she was really there, in Vermillion, Sutton was fast asleep.

CHAPTER TWO

THE NEXT MORNING, Dante was at the bar trying to make sense of the Vine's internet banking, when he heard the front door bump, a half hour before opening time.

He braced, bodily, blood thickening in his veins.

Only instead of a British brunette sidling inside, smiling at him in a way that made him feel an urge to bare his teeth, a big guy in a dirty emergency services uniform sauntered in, strode to the bar, and straddled a stool.

Dante shoved his phone into his back pocket, grabbed a bar towel, and set to wiping down the bench as if punishing the thing. When the customer reached over the counter to grab a donut from beneath the glass cloche, Dante took some solace in smacking the guy's hand with a precise whip of the towel.

"Seriously?" cried Nico, Dante's cousin, cradling his hand, while looking as if he was about to leap over the bar and wrestle Dante to the ground.

Then, realising they were no longer eight years old, Nico went for the donut again instead.

This time Dante let him.

The donuts, and the building in which they resided, belonged to the man after all. The Australian contingent of the Rossi clan owning the Vermillion Hill vineyard and most of Main Street too.

"Where's Chrissy?" Nico asked around a mouthful of pink icing and sprinkles. Then he winced as he lifted the donut to his mouth again.

"Apparently her pet parrot is sick," said Dante, watching his cousin carefully now.

"Chappell or Sabrina?" Nico asked.

Dante hoped his flat stare made it clear he neither knew nor cared. Then when Nico winced again, hissing as he gently rolled his shoulder, Dante asked, "What is wrong?"

"Hmm?"

Dante motioned to Nico's uniform, not liking how beat up it looked. Or the scent of ash Nico brought in with him. Dante had hoped the years he'd spent away from family had inured him to worrying about them, yet his voice was rough as he asked, "Where were you just now? Someplace dangerous? Are you *hurt*?"

Nico cricked his neck. "Nope. Just training."

Dante's hackles shifted from high to medium alert.

His cousin had entertained a knight-in-shining-armour complex since the first time they'd watched *Superman* together as kids. Dante must have been eight, or nine. Nico, a couple of years younger, made a cape out of a tea towel, climbed atop a shed, and tried to fly.

Dante remembered the aftermath—Zia Celia, with Aurora a babe in arms, running after him, screaming, even though Nico had landed in a crouch, then bolted, not a scratch on him. While Isabella—three then, or four—had jumped up and down, cheering him on...

The moment Isabella appeared in his mind's eye, Dante shut the memory down. Before it took him down. Gripping the bar, he wondered what his aunt had been thinking, begging him to leave his sanctuary. What had he been thinking, agreeing?

"Kent!" Nico called, waving a second donut at the bartender, who was chatting up the builder who'd come in early that morning to remove the old cash register.

Kent looked up, smiled, flushed, fixed his hair, and said, "Hey, Nico."

Nico, clearly used to flustering people simply by existing, smiled and asked, "Coffee?"

"Too early, sorry," Kent called back, before glancing at Dante, his smile dropping.

"That your doing?" Nico asked Dante.

"Kent's quivering?"

Nico laughed. "I meant the coffee. But sure.

Let's go with that. Do you always have to be such a surly bastard?"

"Not a case of 'having to be,'" said Dante. "More…preference."

Nico laughed again, only this time on the back of it came a frown. His mouth opened as if about to say more, but then a look came over his face.

The look, Dante called it. The one that told him the exact moment people remembered why he was irascible, how he'd done his best to survive the events that had led to it. Then decided it was best to pretend "the look" hadn't happened at all.

The truth of it was, he was fine with opening the Vine earlier. It could do with a portion of the flourishing Main Street bakery and café crowd. Only Zia Celia had shut the idea down. Cannibalising other businesses who paid them rent apparently not an option.

For someone who had rung him in tears a month ago, begging for his assistance, lest the entire family business collapse, she had plenty of decided opinions now.

"If you disagree with my methods," said Dante, taking a step back, "you're welcome to take my place."

"Ah, no. As you can imagine, I have been forced to work in every part of the family business since birth. We agree my skills are better served elsewhere." With that, Nico swallowed the last mouthful of donut, wiped his hand across the back of his mouth, and stood. "On that note, I am off to see if our tenants need anything fixed, loosened, collected from a high shelf. No rest for the sainted."

With a wide toothy grin, Nico strode to the door, stopping to hold it open when a herd of grey-haired gents wandered inside. He bounced on the spot, a mass of restrained energy, even as he happily chatted to each and every one.

Dante was eighteen months older than Nico, but in that moment it felt like eighteen years; his bones brittle, muscles hardened, mind fractured with bitterness.

Then, Nico looked back at him, clicked his fingers and said, "Hey, did you see the brunette who breezed into town yesterday?"

And Dante's next breath in came quick and sharp.

"Female," Nico, oblivious, went on. "Mid to late twenties. Rented gas-guzzler. Dark sunglasses, dressed all in black. I saw her when I was cruising past Forbidden Fruits."

"Forbidden Fruits?" asked Dante, finally finding his tongue.

Nico's brow lowered, his voice with it. "The R-rated bookstore down the road."

"There's an R-rated bookstore down the road?" one of the older men asked, and the rest stopped and turned.

"Well, not R-rated, exactly," Nico said, looking to Dante for help.

Dante figured he was giving Nico's family more than enough help, so he crossed his arms, and motioned for Nico to go on.

"More *adult*," Nico explained, looking pained. "Spicy, lovey-dovey stuff. Place looks like rainbows and unicorns on the outside but is filled with stories that'd set your hair on fire."

Dante was about to ask how Nico knew what kind of stories they sold, when every one of the older men turned and walked back out the door.

"Wait. Come back!" Nico deplored. "That wasn't an advertisement."

Dante coughed. "Don't need a lack of morning coffee to keep people away, you're doing just fine on your own."

Nico flipped Dante an internationally recognisable hand signal.

When his cousin made to leave, Dante found himself calling out, "So, what did this brunette do? Jaywalk? Murder for hire? Drink an open bottle of non-Vermillion Hill wine in the street?"

Nico rolled his shoulder once more. "Nothing. Yet. Only she and the bookstore owner seemed awfully chummy. In cahoots."

"*Casa è* 'cahoots'?"

"Ah, *combutta*," Nico translated. "*In collusione.* I smell trouble."

Trouble, Dante thought. "Lot of passers-through. Probably long gone by now."

"Probably," Nico agreed, then with a wave over his shoulder, he left.

Only for Sutton Mayberry to walk through the front door of the Vine and Stein not five minutes later.

Her hair was up this time, in a messy bundle atop her head. Her jeans were ripped at the knees, and an oversize Pogues T-shirt and fluffy black cardigan half fell off one shoulder. She was well rumpled, like an unmade bed.

Imagining this woman in bed was enough to set off the claxon inside his head.

Then she looked up, her eyes catching on his. They brightened before a smile followed. Her shoulders lifted in a manner that Dante read, in some deep-down place inside, as delight. Upon spying him.

Dante considered calling Nico, hauling him back so that he might tell this woman the town wasn't big enough for the both of them.

"Hey," said Sutton, pointing at him as if they were old friends.

"Good morning," he said, pointedly, keeping his gaze level, even when her cardigan slipped at her shoulder again.

"I'm not that early, am I?" she asked as she plopped onto a stool, all long limbs and strangely compelling grace.

"You are," he grouched. Even though he'd had

staff set the tables already that day. "What's your excuse?"

"Excuse?" She blinked at him, pink sweeping into her cheeks, as if caught.

Dante pointed to the Wi-Fi sign.

She laughed softly. "Ah, yes. Actually, I was hoping I might be able to set myself up at that table back there again. Only if I'm not in the way. This time I'm paying for the coffee. And one of those donuts would be fabulous."

Dante made to move. Only Kent swept past him, winking as he said, "Stay, keep chatting. I've got this."

"I love super-hot," Sutton said to Kent. "And bitter."

"Amen," said Kent, who kept his head down when Dante shot him a look.

When his gaze once again met Sutton's, her warm eyes smiling up at him, Dante felt as if the floor tipped under him. He pressed his boots harder into the ground and commanded himself to get a grip.

"The B&B is far too quiet to get any work done," said Sutton, leaning on the bar. "I prefer bustle, white noise. I get antsy when it's too quiet. Don't you?"

Dante loved the quiet. Olympic-level quiet. In low season, he'd been known to go days without hearing a voice, not even his own.

Yet, he found himself asking, "So, you *are* staying in town, then?"

She tilted her head in question.

And Dante realised he'd spoken as if she'd been in on Nico's conversation. "We… I assumed you were passing through," he adjusted. Only making it *clear* he'd been thinking of her. Which he had. More than was in any way rational.

A soft smile curled about her lips, before she looked down at her hands, then back up again. "Nope," she said with a shrug. "I'm staying. For a bit. I've taken a room over at the Grape Escape."

Dante nodded, as if he had a clue where that was. He'd worn a path from Vermillion Hill to the Vine and Stein and back again. Seeing no need to venture beyond that route. The sooner he found an answer as to how to make this great white elephant profitable, he'd be on a plane home.

"It is nice there?" he asked, when the alternative was allowing the silence to stretch like a bubble around them.

A sound came from the other end of the bar, where Kent was hovering by the coffee machine as it warmed itself up. A sorry, snorting sound.

"Oh, it's darling," said Sutton, clearly unworried by any of it. "The roof is gabled, so I have to duck if I get too close to the walls. The wallpaper has teeny-tiny grape vines with deer and hedgehogs and rabbits hiding in among the leaves. I've never seen so many scatter cushions in one building, much less one room. But the bed is like a cloud. And the pillows—"

She brought her fingers to her mouth, and sent a kiss into the ether to punctuate her delight.

As Dante's gaze stayed, stuck, on her pouting mouth, a buzzing sound began in the back of his head. When he lifted his gaze, it was to find her eyes on his, the pink in her cheeks a deep rose.

"Anyway," she said, clearing her throat, "*this* place is much more my scene."

"This place?"

She motioned around her.

Dante struggled to believe the Vine with its dark dusty corners, and excess of space, could be anyone's "scene."

"Why is that?" he asked. It was, after all, his duty to wrangle it into profit. Since his suggestions kept getting blowback, outside opinions could not hurt.

"Lots of reasons," she said with a slight shrug, enough that her cardigan slid slowly off her shoulder once more. "The high ceilings. Those gorgeous windows. The great coffee. The potential. I manage indie bands, back in London, so dark and shady, with a dollop of poetic tragedy, is my jam."

She hitched her cardigan sleeve, when it reached her elbow. The roll of her shoulder, the slow stroke of her fingers up her arm so inadvertently sensual Dante pressed his nails into his palms.

"I also love the feeling that if I take up a table

for a couple of hours, I won't be in the way." She said that with a cheeky smile.

Dante grunted in agreement.

"That's a yes?" she asked, sitting taller.

"That table is yours."

"Great!" she said. "Great. Um, should I head over now, or wait here for the coffee and donut—?"

"Go," Dante asserted. "Kent will bring it over."

Kent looked up from the cloche, where he was scooping a donut onto a plate using the supplied tongs. "Are you sure? You can— Nope, seems that's my duty. Hi, I'm Kent."

"Sutton," said Sutton, lifting out of the chair to reach over and shake Kent's hand. "And this time, I'm paying."

Only when Sutton shot them both a smile, then left the bar to make her way to her table did Kent ask, "This time?"

"Long story."

Kent crossed his arms. "I have nothing but time."

Dante's returning look had Kent leaping back to work.

Dante remained behind the counter as Kent delivered Sutton's order. He watched the weak morning sunlight slanting through the large window, raining over Sutton's open laptop, the papers she had stacked on the chair beside her, the wide smile she gave Kent as he slid her plate onto the table, the way she leaned forward sniffing the coffee and grinning.

When his belly contracted with a strange kind of ache, Dante turned away. Once Kent was back behind the counter, he removed himself to the office, where he stayed for the rest of the morning.

It had taken Sutton a minute to remember where she was when she'd woken that morning. Not unusual, considering the number of nights she'd spent in motels, on tour buses, friends of friends' couches.

She'd spotted the brochures on her side table— historical tours, winery visits, forest walks—but it was the Minotaur lamp that had made it all come back to her.

Now, two coffees and two amazing donuts in, she found herself wondering which of the things in the brochures her parents had done together. Had they held hands while walking down Main Street? Made out in the back row of the cinema? Gotten lost together on the way to some waterfall?

Her belly tugged at the thought, only she wasn't sure if it was a *want* to know which of those might be true, or *want*, period.

She'd had relationships, just never *that* kind— all-romance, all-consuming. Far too busy enjoying other big experiences life had to offer. For what if she was anything like her father, and something went wrong…

She shook her head and went back to her laptop. She was making headway on the European summer tour she'd been finagling for the Sweety Pies, a jazz-funk trio she'd discovered a few years before. The logistics of keeping her bands relevant or, better yet, flourishing, kept her more than busy enough.

And boy did Sutton love being busy. No time to think too far into the future when one had to hustle, every single day.

She reached for her coffee. Made and delivered by Kent of the man bun, it was fine, but not quite hot or bitter enough. The one the other guy had made the day before had been far better.

The other guy. Grumpy Bartender.

She couldn't keep calling him that, not if she planned to come in here every day. His name was probably something classic, strong. Giovanni. Or Massimo. Or something deeply poetic, like Romeo. Or...

When her phone—with new Australian sim card installed—rang, Sutton was glad of the distraction.

"Hey!" said Bianca, lead singer of the Magnolia Blossoms—the first band Sutton had ever signed, back when she'd been a restless law student who'd grown up listening to her dad's beloved vinyl collection.

They were also the only one of those early bands she still represented. As great as she was at spotting potential, she was aware of her limitations. As a single-person management team, she was more than happy for them to migrate to larger management groups if they outgrew her. When a tour, or a show, was over, so many of the crew went their separate ways—moving on was a part of the gig.

"Where are you?" Sutton asked, trying to pin the source of the raucous music in the background.

"A punk joint in Leidseplein. Zhou's in the mosh pit. It's chaos!"

Sutton could picture it all too well. After several weeks spent touring small towns throughout Germany and Belgium, the Magnolia Blossoms were spending their autumn in Amsterdam, immersing themselves in the local scene, working on an album, and playing a spate of intimate club shows to test out new sounds.

The rare gap in Sutton's schedule had felt like another sign it was the exact right time for her to finally make the trip to Vermillion.

"So, is wine country adorable as all heck?" Bianca shouted. "Or are you bored out of your mind yet?"

"It's so sweet I'm in constant danger of getting a toothache!" Sutton shouted back, then mouthed an apology when customers a couple of tables over looked her way. Taking her voice down a notch, she said, "Though so far I've spent most of my time in the local pub."

"Naturally. Describe it to me." Bianca was a dedicated aficionado of great venues.

"It's quite a beautiful building, actually. No stage, alas. Kind of feels a little neglected." Sutton looked up, past the heads of the lunchtime crowd starting to fill the tables nearer the bar, to find the Grumpy Bartender was yet to reappear. "There's this bartender—"

"*Now* we're getting somewhere."

"I was going to say he makes great coffee."

"Honey, we've known enough bartenders in our time to know it's never about how well they pour drinks."

Bianca had a point. Bartenders were often consummate flirts, but the hulking Italian was not of that ilk. In fact, she couldn't quite pin what ilk he was. She'd always been a fast judge of character, had to be in order to keep up with the flimflam she dealt with in her line of work, but he was hard to pin down.

Not that she wanted to pin him, down or otherwise.

"This bartender makes superb coffee and is a total grouch," she blurted as she tried to wipe *that* image out of her mind.

"Sutton's got a cru-ush!"

"Please," she said, but it was a half-hearted effort. "The man looks at me like he's wondering what I taste like."

A beat later, Bianca made a choking sound.

Then Sutton heard her yell, relaying the information to someone nearby in a very loud voice.

"Gimme the phone," a new voice said. Francie, the Magnolia Blossoms' bass player. "Was there a piano involved when this tasting occurred? I always love a piano scene."

"What? No!" Realising she was all but shouting again, Sutton ducked her head and pressed her mouth to the phone. "I meant in a big bad wolf kind of way. And there's no piano here that I can see."

Though one would fit nicely in the back corner, she thought.

She really should cool it with the fairy tale angle. Her parents had been all about that—eyes meeting across a crowded room, et cetera. And while for her father, being so drawn to her mother was a highlight of his life, Sutton couldn't see how it was worth the pain of what came after.

Not that she was *drawn to* the Grumpy Bartender. Except, considering how much bandwidth she'd given the man, maybe she sort of was.

If something romantically inclined *were* to happen to her while she was in the town in which her parents had fallen in love, was that an objectively bad thing? Or the perfect place to open herself up to the one great adventure she'd steadfastly avoided thus far?

The thing was, while she'd found herself thinking about his large hands, and rough stubble, he'd neither said nor done a single thing to make her think such thoughts went both ways.

Flattened by that realisation, Sutton said, "Now the club, the Liefdescafé—are you happy with the setup? Anything you need me to manage?"

Bianca gave Sutton the rundown of the series of shows they'd contracted to play in a fabulously cool club on the bank of the Amstel over the northern autumn. Only Sutton found herself listening with half an ear as Grumpy Bartender appeared behind the bar.

Kent of the man bun and the blue-haired pixie with the undercut and sleeve tattoos listened intently as his hands cut through the air in that elegantly expressive manner Italians seemed to be born with.

"Have you told your dad where you are yet?"

Sutton blinked back into her conversation. Bianca had met her dad, adored her dad, and understood the complication. "Not yet."

"Just tell him you've met a grumpy bartender who works in a run-down bar but owns no piano. He'll be on cloud nine."

Sutton let her face fall into her hand, as she pictured her father with a hopeful smile on his face. He was so proud of her work, but didn't understand that looking for "the one" had never been her driving force. She could hardly tell him he was the reason why.

Just then, Sutton spied a familiar blonde in a

poison-green '50s sundress hovering near the Vine's front door. Laila of the spicy fairy bookstore. Laila to whom she'd promised to buy lunch.

"Bianca," said Sutton, pushing back her chair. "I have to go. Liefdescafé follow-up tomorrow, okay?"

Hand over her eyes as if she was squinting into the abyss, Laila spotted Sutton, waved, then made a beeline.

Bianca rang off as Laila reached the table. After air kisses, and hellos, Laila sat down, dumped the book she'd been carrying on the table. Sutton side-eyed the muscular half man, half bear clinging to a lithe young woman in a torn dress on the cover, while Laila looked around as if waiting for the boogeyman to jump out from behind a table.

"So," said Laila without preamble, "you know the man who has been trying to make me change the name of my store? He came into Forbidden Fruits this morning, with another 'perfect alternative' for the name of my haven for women who own their desires. Wait for it." Laila held up both hands. "Stories with a Side of Shiraz."

Sutton coughed out a laugh.

"I'd like to give him a 'side of shiraz,'" Laila muttered. Then, "Anyway, his name is Niccolo Rossi. The Rossi family own this place, as well as the vineyard up on the hill. They own the entire town, practically. The punny shop names is *their* thing—a way to create a point of difference from the high-tech grape regions nearby, the German strongholds, and the venerable old-money labels."

"Sounds positively feudal."

"Right? A grape is a grape is a grape as far as I'm concerned. A cocktail, on the other hand, now that's something worth crowing about."

"Fair," said Sutton. "But you have to admit this building is pretty wonderful. So atmospheric. The architectural detail is gorgeous."

Laila looked around. "Agree to disagree. Now, who do I have to do to get a coffee around here?"

Sutton's gaze went straight to the bar. Only to find Grumpy Bartender watching her. Even when he shifted and looked away almost instantly, she felt the touch of his gaze like a sunburn.

"Ah," said Laila, twisting on the chair. "The 'architectural detail.' Now I get it."

Laila held up a hand, miming a request for a menu, then turned back to Sutton. "Now, before the hot woodchopper lumbers over here, let's get straight to it. I prefer keeping my 'back in ten minutes' sign up at the bookshop for half an hour, max."

"Okay," said Sutton, along for the ride now. Especially if the universe was about to put some new venture in her path. "Let's."

Laila sat forward, holding Sutton's gaze as if about to give her the answer to life, the universe, and everything. "We had not known one another five minutes before you told me three things—

you had come halfway across the world, you were single, and this was where your parents met and fell in love."

Sutton was pretty sure she'd said other things too, but Laila was clearly following a thought.

"I believe," said Laila, "that's because you are hoping lightning will strike in the same place twice."

"By lightning you mean…?"

"Love lightning!" Laila said, her expression making it clear Sutton was acting dim. "You are craving it. I can see it written all over your face."

Sutton placed both hands on her cheeks. While *craving* was a strong word, she couldn't help remembering the strange sense of longing she'd felt, imagining her parents walking the same footsteps. Together.

"*This* is where it's going to happen for you, Sutton. I can feel it." Laila looked around, and shuddered. "Well, maybe not *this* place, but this general geographical area."

Sutton knew she could shoot down Laila's theory—claim nostalgia, a love of adventure, any number of excuses for making the trip. But what if that's all they were—excuses?

The ticking clock, her mother's age when she'd died, her lifelong desire to squeeze every ounce out of the opportunities her life gave her—that *had* led her to this place. Stuck with the truth that the only one of life's greatest adventures that she'd deliberately avoided was opening herself up to the possibility of falling in love.

Belly filled with butterflies, Sutton shuffled to the front of her chair, and kept her voice low. "Could you really see all that in me?"

Laila smiled. "Honey, however many romance novels you think I've read in my lifetime, triple it. The signs are all there. The stars have aligned. Consider me your fairy godmother."

"So, what are you suggesting I do about this… this love lightning?" Sutton asked, right as a shadow fell over the table.

She looked up to find the Grumpy Bartender looming over them, holding a pair of menus. He refused to meet her eye, as if he'd heard every word of her last sentence.

"Why, hello," Laila said, holding out a hand, palm down, as if waiting for the thing to be kissed. "I'm Laila Vale. And who might you be?"

Grumpy Bartender's right eyebrow flickered north. "Dante," he said in that deep rough burr of a voice. "Dante Rossi."

So, his name is Dante, Sutton thought. Then, *Of course it is.*

"You're a Rossi?" said Laila, pulling back her hand. "Related to *Niccolo*, I presume? Yes, I see it now. In the eyes. The stubborn jawline. The air of entitlement."

Lines formed around Dante's warm brown eyes and for a second Sutton thought he might actually smile. In the end he merely huffed out a hard-done-by sigh. "Nico is my cousin," he said. "Younger. Do not hold it against me."

Laila perked up. "I'll consider it." Then she held up a finger as she looked at the menu.

When Dante the Grumpy Bartender waited, impatience rolling from him like a fog, and still he did not look her way, Sutton might have felt miffed, if not for the chance it gave her to take him in.

With the sunlight slanting over half his face, he looked like something out of a Michelangelo painting. If he lost the flannel button-down shirt, and dark jeans, that was. Not that Sutton was picturing how he might look minus shirt and jeans. Only now that she'd thought it, she was. In rather impressive detail. She imagined he'd be hard, beneath the clothes, bulky, all slabs of muscle, enough that she was left feeling hot and sparky and all kinds of upended.

"Flat white," said Laila, eventually. "Drizzle of caramel, whipped cream on top." She held out her menu and Dante took it.

Sutton opened her mouth to quickly request coffee number three.

Only for Dante to say, "Yet another espresso for you?"

The fact that he still did not look her way set something off inside her. "That all depends."

And Dante's gaze finally slid to hers. If she

thought she'd felt a case of sunburn earlier, it was nothing compared with the heat that crawled into her face in that moment.

"On?" he asked, somehow making the word last longer than it had any right to last.

She leaned forward, resting her chin in her palm, and said, "Who's making it?"

His brow knitted, all "bear disturbed in the middle of a long winter sleep." Then he flicked his hair from his face, in a way that deserved to be in slow mo. "Would you care to put in a request?"

"Kent tried, twice. But they had nothing on the one you made for me yesterday."

Dante tucked the menu beneath his arm, and turned to face her more fully. "You are ruining your taste buds, you know."

"Lucky for me, they're mine to ruin."

The deep frown was back, the one that said "I am here under protest." Only this time she swore she saw a spark in his eyes. Heat. The thrill of the battle.

When he turned to leave, she found herself saying, "Thanks, Dante."

He paused, emitted a sound much like a growl, then stalked away.

It wasn't until he had made it all the way back behind the bar, where he ignored someone asking for assistance, instead moving straight to the coffee machine, that Laila spoke up.

"Pass me a fan, because what was *that*?"

"That was *Dante*," Sutton said on an outshot of breath.

"Oh, no," Laila said, eyes bright, "that was a whole lot of hot, yearning, deeply delicious flirtation, threatening to set this place alight."

Sutton blinked, then reached over and picked up Laila's book. "I think you've read too many romance novels."

"There is no such thing as too many romance novels," Laila assured her. "Now, if you're sure you've not already been struck—"

Sutton shook her head, heartily enough that Laila stopped midsentence. And Laila kindly didn't make some comment about her protesting too much.

"Okay, then. Back to Mission: Find Sutton's Love Lightning."

"Ironic, I know, but any chance we can change the name?"

"Fine. But no wine puns."

"Deal. So, where do you imagine we start?"

"We start by hosting the biggest singles night this PG town has ever seen!"

CHAPTER THREE

"A SINGLES NIGHT," Sutton repeated, feeling a flicker of excitement. Or was it dread?

"It is literally the best idea I've had in ages," Laila gushed. "And that's saying something. You will find the perfect someone with whom to embark on a grand love affair. I will expand my mailing list. Win-win."

Sutton laughed. "You're not doing this for your *mailing list.*"

"I'm a single business owner. Don't mock the mailing list."

Sutton gave her a look.

"Fine." Laila's shoulders slumped. "I'm not a complete mercenary. I'm relatively new to this town and while the business is going pretty great, meeting other locals, my age, with similar interests, would be nice."

That Sutton understood. "I'm in!" she said. "If only to help you make friends."

Laila poked out her tongue, then realised Sutton had agreed to her plan. "Oh, my gosh! We're doing this!"

Laila went on to talk crowd—half her customers were tourists, a good portion regular visitors from Adelaide way. "We are ripe with backpackers on working visas, and I imagine there are any number of lonely grape farmers...or whatever one calls them. As for location—I've considered hosting at Forbidden Fruits, but we are on the cosy side and I have no desire to have my wares pawed over by nonbelievers."

"What about here?" Sutton asked.

Laila screwed up her nose. "Very funny."

"I mean it," Sutton said, feeling definite excitement now. "Picture it, the tables all moved to the sides, opening up the centre for people to mill, gather, maybe even dance. Music playing from hidden speakers, warm faux candlelight everywhere glinting against the windows, the polished wood floor. I wonder if we can get them to drop the chandeliers, all tucked up into that high ceiling."

Sutton again imagined a stage at the far end of the space. There'd be room behind for storage and green rooms. Speakers and lighting rigs above. The roof was high enough they could easily add a mezzanine...

Okay, so not *now*. But it was something the place should consider.

"Lean into the dark and seedy?" said Laila. "It would add a certain edge to the event. In fact, it could be kind of fabulous. Okay, I'll take charge of the invites, and since you're friendly with management, you can look after logistics."

Sutton came back into her own body with a *phwump*. "Friendly? I wouldn't go that far."

Laila grinned. "Friendly/circling one another with lust in your eyes. Tom-ay-to tom-ah-to." Then, "Of course, if you're hesitating because you already have your eye on a certain lumberjack, then—"

"No," Sutton said. "I don't. It's not… It's fine."

Laila leaned forward, her cool hand wrapping around Sutton's warm one. "You are about to meet the man of your dreams. I will make a million new friends. If not, then at least we can both score great shags we can look back on in our old age with fondness."

And that was when Kent appeared then with their coffees. He placed Laila's down first, a grin hovering at the corner of his mouth.

"You know what?" said Laila, looking at her phone. "I'm going to have to take this to go."

Kent looked at the fancy swirl of whipped cream atop the thing, imagining getting it into a takeaway cup, and winced.

"It all looks the same once it hits your belly," said Laila, gathering her things. "Lock this place in, Sutton. No time to lose. This is going to be the wildest thing this town has seen in years."

"Wildest thing?" Kent asked, watching Laila sashay toward the bar with her mug.

"It seems we are hosting a singles night," Sutton said.

"Where and when?"

"Soon. We're hoping here."

Kent's smile dropped. "Good luck with *that*. Then again…" He glanced over his shoulder before putting Sutton's coffee in front of her. "He did make your coffee twice, to make sure he got it just right."

"He…" Sutton looked up to find Dante behind the bar. "He did not."

"Cross my heart," Kent sing-songed as he backed away. "Get this thing off the ground and count me in."

Sutton could only offer a quick thumbs-up.

It was a little over twenty-four hours since she'd arrived in Vermillion, and she'd been assured of a "grand love affair" if not love lightning. While it all sounded fantastical the moment she wasn't caught up in Laila's vortex, now that it was out there, in the universe, she could feel the pull of it, tugging her in that direction.

She hadn't realised she was staring into the middle distance until her focus cleared to find Dante watching her, again.

She lifted his coffee to her mouth, took a sip, found the flavour strong, lush, just on the verge of hot, but not enough to sear. It was gorgeous.

Dante cocked his head in question.

Sutton smiled, and mouthed, *Perfect*.

Dante nodded. Then for the longest of moments, they simply looked at one another.

When someone stepped up to the bar, and eye contact was lost, Sutton slumped back in her chair. That man was most definitely not on her list of possibilities—she was considering dipping a toe into romantic waters, not diving off a cliff.

Dante lay on the couch in Chrissy's office, eyes closed, feet hanging off the edge. Dean Martin crooned softly from a record player atop the filing cabinet, as Dante attempted to give his mind a five-minute reprieve.

He'd been in Vermillion for over two weeks, and the light still felt wrong, the air smelled different, the tap water tasted strange. Sleep had been hard to come by. And whatever bad thoughts might plague a person in daylight, without distraction they only came back louder at night.

He shifted so that his shoulders found a slightly less uncomfortable spot, breathed out, breathed in, long and slow, an approach to quieting the mind he'd found online late one night. Thankfully, the clouds of rest began to infuse the edges of his vision—

"Oh, sorry," a voice cut through the fog.

Dante opened his eyes. Slowly. Moving the arm over his eyes to cradle his head, he looked to find Sutton Mayberry standing in the office doorway.

As ever, the mere sight of her did something

to him. Her loveliness, her *vitalità*, the fact she kept showing up—whatever it was, strong, physical reactions stirred in him when she was near. He fought them, gamely, as one song ended, the needle sliding into a groove between songs, and another began.

"Can I help you?" Dante asked, expecting she'd taken a wrong turn.

"I… Chrissy sent me back here."

Did she, now? The fact that he'd given Chrissy an official warning for arriving late, again, that morning a likely cause.

With a groan, Dante curled himself to sitting, then reached over to turn off the record player. The sudden silence in the room felt heavy, weighted, as if without it there was no masking the tension between them.

When he looked up, it was to find she'd not moved. In fact, she was white-knuckling the doorjamb, her gaze zeroed in on his chest.

He looked down. Ah, the bright purple T-shirt sporting the Vine and Stein logo into which he'd been forced to change, after one of the kitchen staff had walked through the wrong kitchen swing door, running smack bang into him, planting a plate of pasta to his chest. His backup shirt having been utilized the day before, he'd had no choice but to rummage through an old box of uniforms he'd found in the corner. The thing was a good two sizes too small.

Running a hand through his hair, he looked up again to find Sutton still staring. And something came over him, some gremlin making him sit a little taller, roll his shoulders. He might even have flexed, just a smidge.

Her mouth popped open on an outshot of breath. Which told him all he needed to know, and far more than he wanted to. Which was that this tension, this wild energy he felt in her presence, was not only on him.

"Sutton," he growled.

She blinked, furiously, her gaze lifting guilty to his. "Sorry, you were clearly taking a break. I'll come back later."

"No," he said. No point now. He went to ask again what she wanted, when the office landline rang. He waited for someone out front to pick it up. And waited.

"Scusi," he apologised, then, standing, picked up the phone and barked, *"Pronto."*

"Dante! So nice to hear your lovely voice," his aunt cooed with beautifully couched sarcasm, before tripping into instant Italian. She asked after his day, asked if he'd seen Niccolo, told him Zia Carlotta, in Sicily, a relation he'd never heard of, had come through her operation. She chatted as if this was how things had always been. As if he'd not been a family pariah for over a decade.

This he noted absently, distracted as he was by the sight of Sutton now moving about the space.

Her fingers running over open boxes of cardboard cups, teetering piles of napkins, she paused at the box of purple Vine and Stein shirts, then moved to glance over the swathes of paper on the desk.

She stopped in front of the wall covered in old band flyers, Post-it notes so ancient they were curling at the corners, and the large, framed aerial photograph of Vigna dell'Essenza, the very first Rossi family vineyard, where he and Isabella had grown up.

When she moved past it, Dante let out a ragged breath.

When she reached the record player, she looked to him, asked with her eyes if she could start it up again. He nodded, and Dean was back.

She flicked through the box of old vinyls— all Italian, or Italian-adjacent. She pulled one from the box, gaze roving over the old-fashioned font and imagery. Her bottom lip, he noted, was slightly fuller than the top. Her nose had a slight bump on the end. Her hair was a sun-kissed dark brown.

He wondered if the monastic silence had not been safer than having "Memories Are Made of This" as the soundtrack to his wayward thoughts.

"Dante!" his aunt chided, as if it wasn't the first time she'd said his name.

"Si."

Then, in English, "Are you the one with the mushroom allergy?"

"No," he said. "That was Isabella."

The moment the words were out of his mouth his aunt made a sound, a kind of gasp and gulp in one. A sound that had haunted him enough that he'd left his entire family behind so that he'd not have to hear it again.

"No matter. *Non ci sarò per cena*," he said. He would not be back for dinner. For he would not walk through the door and see the apology, the agony, in his aunt's face.

"I must get back to work. *Ciao*," he said, then hung up the phone.

Pulse thudding behind his ears, he placed the phone in the cradle, and rubbed both hands over his face, before delving them into his hair. When he looked up, Sutton was watching him, her expression curious. Concerned.

Blood up, he snarled, "Why did Chrissy send you back here?"

"Because I asked where you were," she shot back, as if she'd felt the chill in the air and refused to let him turn it on her.

She slid the record back into the box, then leaned back against the filing cabinet, crossing her arms. "Where *will* you be?"

"Scusi?"

"You told your…your friend that you won't be home for dinner."

"Not *home*," he said. Home was a long way away. "I told my *aunt*, to whom I was speaking, I won't be eating at hers tonight." Then, "You speak Italian?"

"*Un po'*," she said, holding two fingers close together. "I'm a band manager, so lots of back-road European tours. Small venues in out-of-the-way towns where not everyone is able, or willing, to speak English. One of my bass players—Francie from the Magnolia Blossoms—is from Positano, so we've toured Italy quite a bit."

"What does a band manager do?" he asked, glad to move the subject on.

"Different things on different days. Line up gigs, marketing, negotiating contracts, schmoozing, strong-arming bar managers." She shot him a quick smile. "I can be very persuasive on that score."

As he well knew. "And you can do all that," he asked, "from a table by the window?"

"I can do it anywhere."

Her eyes flickered as the accidental double entendre bounced between them, and something dark shifted beneath Dante's sternum. Like a great dragon that had lain slumbering through a century-long winter, wakening after a deep sleep.

Yet rather than end this—for the longer she stayed, the more things she touched, the more of her energy, her scent, she would leave behind— he found himself saying: "You do know that nobody is actually *from* Positano."

Sutton blinked, then burst into laughter. The

sound husky, bringing with it a wide smile that sparked glints in her night-dark eyes. "That's gold. I've met Francie's family, by the way, in their home, in Positano, but I am so saving that. It'll make her head explode. Are you from near there? Originally, I mean."

"Siena," he said, glancing at the framed photograph of Vigna dell'Essenza before he could stop himself. The hills, the driveway lined with pencil pines, the villa with its brick red roof—the likes of it could be found all over Italy. But this configuration any Rossi would recognise as theirs.

At the edge of the shot was the very tip of a dam. It was enough for Dante to look away.

"Now," he said, "my home is Montefalco, in Umbria."

"So, you don't live here, then? In Australia."

"I do not." He could have stopped there, but that face, those warm eyes compelled him to add, "I'm here helping family. Once my work is done, I will be gone."

Her brow knitted a moment, before she began moving about the room once more. "So, if you are not a South Australian pub manager, what is it that you do?"

"I make wine."

"Plenty of vineyards around here, I've noticed."

"Not like mine."

"How so?"

"Different grapes, different varietals, different

history. Different seasons and soil, sunrises and sunsets, rainfall and timing. Different levels of management expertise."

"So, a grape is not simply a grape."

"A grape is not simple at all."

"No?" she said.

And if he was not so attuned to the slightest movements in her expression, he might have missed the teasing note in her eyes. Might not have felt the tap of it against his chest, and the warmth that spread from that point out to his very extremities.

Choosing to take her question at face value, he explained, "We grow several varietals at Sorello— my vineyard—the primary being the Sagrantino, a grape indigenous to the region. It flowers early, yet requires a long, hot season if it is to ripen as we'd like. Low-yielding, thick-skinned, broody, high tannins—picked too soon it leaves the mouth grippy, dry. Yet when nursed into perfect fruition, it yields the lushest inky, earthy, plummy delight."

Her tongue darted out to wet her lower lip before she dragged her teeth over the spot. "Sounds yummy."

"Yummy," he repeated, gaze caught on the sheen on that bottom lip. Plump, lovely. Off-limits.

"I can only assume so," she said, "since you looked like you were having a religious experience just now."

He looked up, humbled by what his expression must have given away.

"I'm not a wine drinker," she said with a shrug. "So, I wouldn't know."

Dante breathed out in relief. She'd been referring to his enthusiasm when talking about wine, not when his attention had been on her mouth. Only... Back up a moment.

"Did you just say you are *not a wine drinker*?"

"Yep."

He leaned against the back of the couch. "By that you mean you are no expert?"

"By that I mean I drink coffee. Lager, when out. Cocktails on occasion. I've tried wine, but to me it tastes kind of...sour."

Dante's hands lifted in the air before floating back to grip the chair. Such words from anyone else would feel like a knife to the heart, but the way the woman drank coffee, she clearly did not know what she was missing.

"I could change your mind," he said.

She looked over her shoulder, her gaze connecting with his. "My will is strong, and I know what I like."

The words *lasciami provare* tripped to the edge of his tongue. *Let me try.* He swallowed them back, teetering between knowing his limits and wanting things he simply could not have.

She held out her hands in surrender. "I'm sure your wine is amazing, in the grand scheme of wines. I can't imagine it would dare be anything less, with you in charge."

Dante bowed, accepting her words as true.

Then she smiled, nose scrunching up at the edges, lines fanning from the edges of her eyes. It looked so right on her it was clear she smiled a lot.

"Sutton," he said.

"Yes?" she said, adding "Dante," a beat later.

And the dragon inside him roared.

"Why did you come find me?" he asked.

Her eyes widened. "Right! I have a proposal for you. Well, for the manager of this place. Which I've just discovered is *not* you."

"It is not," he assured her. "And yet, propose away."

He folded his arms, noted the way her gaze dropped to his biceps, where the sleeve of the too-small T-shirt cut into his flesh. This time he did not flex. He was not Nico, prancing about like he was Prince of Vermillion. In fact, he could shake his cousin right about now, off as he was playing firefighter/cop/mayor/whatever fantasy he was living out rather than doing his duty by his family so that Dante could do as he pleased.

"Prepare yourself," said Sutton, hands out, as if readying to sell him something, "I do believe I have found a way to pay you back for letting me set up a work base here."

"I did not realise that is what I had done."

She waved a hand at him, as if he'd made a

great joke. Then hit him with, "What do you say to the Vine and Stein hosting a singles night?"

"A what?"

"A singles night! An event where people who are unattached mingle and meet. Ticketed. Tickets get them entry, nibbles and first drink. Cash bar after that, of which we take a percentage. Or we take ticket sales, you take the booze. All negotiable. We hire a band—"

She seemed to check herself there. "You're not set up for a band. I can source a sound system. We play great music. Make it a Saturday night, seven till eleven. Long enough to pack them in, not so long you have to pay too much overtime."

"Overtime?"

"You'll *have* to put on extra staff."

"Whatever for?"

She looked at him as if wondering if he'd heard a word. "To cater for the customers. Who would come. To the singles night."

"Did you not say, yesterday, that you had not long arrived in the country? And you came up with this idea when?"

"My part in the planning has covered maybe the last hour, or two." Then, "The idea was Laila's—she runs Forbidden Fruits, the local bookstore, and has been thinking about it for some time."

Ah. The R-rated joint that had Nico all het up. The idea suddenly became all the more interesting. "Why?"

"Laila is certain it will drum up business for the entire strip."

"No. Why you?"

Sutton nibbled at the inside of her lip, her cheeks pinking, then she looked away, then down at her hands, then back at him. Gaze beseeching. And it hit him.

"*You* are hoping to meet someone at this... *singles* night?"

"Me?" Her hand flew to her chest, pink blotches now creeping down her neck. "No. I mean, sure. Meeting people is a nice thing, don't you think?"

Dante did not.

"But... That's not *why*. I'm in Vermillion, as it's where my parents met. So maybe I'm trying to find a connection to them here, somehow? I honestly don't know." She wrinkled her nose, as if the whole thing made her feel uncomfortable. Then shook it off and said, "Anyway, if we do this thing, you'd be most welcome to sign up too. To meet *other* people, I mean. Because we've already met. Not that you and I... I mean, if you're even single, that is."

She swallowed, as if waiting for him to confirm or deny. He said nothing. Interested to see where her flusters might lead the conversation.

Then she held out both hands and breathed out hard. "Short answer—*life's* short. When I get the impetus to do something, I don't muck about. So, what do you say? Wanna help us do this thing?"

Having spent the past decade hardening himself to wanting anything more than he already had, having Sutton Mayberry ask him what he wanted felt treacherous. But his duty was to wrestle the Vine and Stein into the black, and Sutton had just offered up a big step toward doing just that.

As if she could sense his defences melting, she smiled warmly, and said, *"Bene?"*

"Sì. Bene."

She clapped her hands, and jumped up and down on the spot. Then, before he felt her move, she took a large step and threw her arms around his neck. Enveloping him in a hug.

As he was leaning against the back of the couch, he reached for her so she'd not topple them both backward; hands landing on her waist, gathering handfuls of soft T-shirt.

Time slowed in an instant—he could feel the shift of her as she breathed, the warmth of her skin through her thin T-shirt. Her hair, soft as silk, tickled his cheek, a soft puff of her breath kissed his ear.

How long had it been since someone had held him this way? Not a welcome kiss from family, or a meaningless night in the bed of a stranger. But held with intent. Such joy.

He drank it in, absorbing her vitality as if it had the power to recharge him for life. Until, in the moment when it would have felt most natural for

her to pull away, her arms tightened. Incrementally. Ruinously.

Before he even felt himself move, Dante's
hands shifted, sliding around her, gathering her
shirt, fingertips tracing the curve of her back, the
bumps of her spine, as he pulled her danger close.

While a small voice in the back of his brain
tried desperately to get his attention, to warn him
to stop, he felt the change in her too. The way she
softened against him, her breasts pressing into his
chest, the curl of her fingers as they slid up his
neck and into his hair—

Then suddenly she leaped away. Ruffling a
hand through her hair, tugging at her T-shirt,
spinning in a circle.

Dante's hands hovered, midair, reaching for
what they'd lost, before he drew them back. His
blood thrummed through him, a heavy pulsing
beat that made his ears ring, and his chest burn.

"Anyway, I'll go now," she said. "Get the ball
rolling. It'll be great. Amazing. Big success.
Thank you." She looked up at him then, eyes a
swirl of heat and confusion.

Then she held out a fist, begging for a bump. As
if that might erase the intimacy of their embrace.

With a soft laugh, he gave her what she needed.
When their knuckles knocked, a spark of electricity leaped from her hand to his, or vice versa. Her
eyes snapped to his and he knew she felt it too.

Around the couch she bolted, then out the door shouting, "You won't regret this!"

As Dante stood on legs that weren't altogether steady, flooded with thoughts and feelings too frantic to push down deep, he already did.

CHAPTER FOUR

THE AIR WAS cool and fresh, the leaves sparkled with morning dew not yet burned away by the spring sunshine.

Sutton stepped over a lichen-covered log, lamenting her Vans probably weren't the most appropriate footwear for a bush walk, but the Stringybark Loop Hike had been labelled "lightly undulating," and was the shortest trail in Barry's brochures, so it was what it was.

"Why are we doing this?" asked Laila, who was several steps behind, brushing a spiky-leaved bush so it didn't attack her legs.

"Two birds," said Sutton, "one stone."

Laila pressed her heart-shaped sunglasses higher on her nose. "The rare chance your parents walked this path together is not a 'bird.' It's guesswork. Why not call your dad and ask, and next time don't invite me."

Ignoring that perfectly sensible option, Sutton waited for Laila to catch up. "You've lived here, what, a few months now? And you've never done anything on Barry's brochures. If you want to be a part of this community, I think it'll take more than a singles night."

Laila harrumphed. Literally.

"My dad likes walks," said Sutton, as she started up again. "He'd have found these trails for sure."

In fact, Sutton had found him perusing a website about a walking tour in Devon the last time she'd visited. When she'd hinted that maybe Marjorie, his lovely neighbour who gladly checked in on her father when Sutton was away, might enjoy the website too, he'd shut it down and changed the subject entirely.

"And your mother?" Laila asked.

"I actually don't know. Dad's stories are more about that first flush of love, then there's a gap, then it's all about me."

"Hmm. Time to turn around—I only have a half hour till the store opens."

Sutton turned and followed Laila back down the "hill." "A lot of people get the urge to buy Viking romance at eight thirty on a Wednesday morning?"

"It's not about the customers. It's about the books. They miss me."

"Second bird, then," said Sutton. "I spoke to Dante."

Laila caught up faster than a person in wedge heels on a hiking path ought to be able. "And?"

"The Vine and Stein is a go."

"Yes!" said Laila. "How did you convince him? Seduce him with your vixen wiles?"

"I asked. It was that simple."

Though walking in on him sprawled on the small couch like a slain giant had felt anything but simple. The tight purple T-shirt had proved any imaginings she'd had about what he might look like sans flannel shirts and jeans had not done the man justice. Then there was the tattoo—delicate tendrils of what must be grape vines curling out the bottom of the T-shirt sleeve. Working in the indie music scene, she'd seen more tattooed skin than not, yet she'd spent more time than she'd care to admit thinking about Dante's, wondering how far it went—over his shoulder, up his neck, down his back, lower?

"Well, colour me happy," said Laila. "Not only because we have a venue but because I do believe we are at the end of this thing."

Laila all but skipped the final few metres of the trail, patted the sign, and made her way to Sutton's rental car.

On the ten-minute drive back to Vermillion, they talked through ideas for how they could deck out the Vine, what the invitations ought to look like, getting-to-know-you games the attendees could play.

"It's official," Laila declared. "Dante Rossi is officially my favourite Rossi."

"I've not met any others, so have nothing to compare him with."

A quick glance sideways showed Laila's smile was slow and wide. "Oh, honey, you don't need to meet the rest to know he's the one for you."

"I thought we'd established he was off the table."

"Meh. It's a woman's prerogative to change her mind."

When Laila pulled out her phone to start making a music playlist for the night, Sutton wondered what Laila might say if she told her what had happened *after* Dante had said yes.

Music people were touchy-feely—sharing dressing rooms and cramped tour buses, lots of sitting on laps in backs of cars. But hugging Dante, holding Dante, had felt nothing like that.

There was the sound he'd made, a kind of soul-deep murmur. The feel of those big hands on her waist, rough skin catching on her shirt, long fingers spanning her like it was nothing. It was foolish and deeply intimate. And if she'd used it as a form of self-help to get to sleep that night, well that was her own private Idaho.

"Penny for your thoughts," said Laila, radar clearly pinging.

Sutton quickly pointed to the rows of red rose bushes along the outskirts of yet another vineyard, meaning the turnoff to Vermillion was close. "Did you know the roses are an early warning system? They attract aphids and contract diseases, such as black rot, before vines do. Read it in a brochure."

"Look at you being a good little tourist."

"I really am. Drop you at the shop?"

"Perfection. Let's do dinner at the Vine tonight so we can sort out next steps. Say eight?"

"Sure thing." Sutton tapped her fingers on the steering wheel as she pictured walking into the place at night, Dante behind the bar, those hot dark eyes hitting her like a laser beam. "Though we can go somewhere different, if you prefer?"

"And lose traction? Not a chance. Unless there's a very good reason why you'd like to take a breather?"

"Nope! The Vine is fine."

"The 'Vine' is fine indeed."

After Sutton dropped Laila off, she made her way back to the B&B, had a shower, got changed, and listened to a couple of demo playlists she'd been sent. Nearing lunchtime, she grabbed her laptop, and went to head out, only to pause at the door.

Maybe she'd go see a matinee at the local cinema instead.

Was she being a big chicken? Yes.

Could she live with herself? Again, yes.

Throwing herself into Dante's arms in a moment of delight had been one thing, but shoving herself under his nose multiple times a day would absolutely give him the wrong idea.

Best keep some space between. For the way he told it, he was leaving any day now, and the man was the proverbial bear with a thorn in his paw, and she'd not come to Vermillion to get distracted trying to figure out how to remove someone else's ouch, when she had her own stuff to figure out.

And if she kept making excuses *not* to see him, even she'd stop believing she meant it.

For once, Chrissy was early, Kent was in a great mood, and nothing went wrong in the kitchen. The place was even a smidge busier than usual. Yet from just before opening, and all day since, Dante had felt as if his insides were tied in knots.

All because he was waiting for a certain brunette to come walking through his door. To order her horrendous excuse for a coffee, and take her place at the table by the last window, where he'd ordered Kent to place a reserved sign that had stayed there all damn day because she'd never come.

He looked at his watch to see it was a little after eight. Late enough he'd have missed dinner with his aunt, again, and would have to grab a plate of something from the kitchen. After which he'd slink into the guesthouse on the hill, and fall into bed, hopefully exhausted enough to sleep a dreamless sleep.

He'd not seen his aunt since his slip the day before. Or spoken to her since saying Isabella's name. He knew it had provided an opening, and he did not want to have that talk. He'd heard it all. How much they all still missed her. How the tragedy might have been avoided if they'd both been given stronger guidance from their father. How it wasn't Dante's fault.

Leaving Vigna dell'Essenza and turning his back on the family business had been a means of survival. Sorello would never reach the level of Rossi Wines' success, but it was lucrative, and gratifying, and enough to curate his own reputation as a master winemaker.

He'd built a life good enough to sustain him and those who relied on him, but not so much blue sky the guilt of it ate him alive. The balance was finespun, and he would not allow it to become unhinged.

Then, as if the gods had been listening, the door to the Vine opened, bringing with it a wash of cool night air and Sutton Mayberry. A wave of longing rushed over him with such haste, such violence, he had to remind himself to breathe.

Sutton glanced around, as if searching for someone. When her gaze found him, her mouth dropped open, her chest rose and fell. As if she too found herself having to battle that same rogue wave.

"Sutton!" said Kent, moving in beside Dante. So wound up was he, he flinched.

With a deep, fortifying breath, Sutton walked to the bar. "Hey, Kent. Dante."

Dante nodded.

"We were waiting all day for you to come," Kent went on. "We were worried something was wrong." Kent looked to Dante as if assuming he'd back that up.

Dante had no intention of letting Sutton Mayberry know that he'd thought of her at all. The way she felt in his arms. How the scent of her on his skin had lingered for hours.

"I'm great. Spent the day playing tourist. Now I'm meeting someone for dinner. Laila, from the bookstore. We're meeting to talk about singles night."

"It's happening?" Kent asked.

"It's happening."

Kent held out a fist, which Sutton leaned in to bump.

Then her eyes snapped to Dante's, and he knew she was remembering the moment they'd bumped fists the day before. And all that had led to it.

Tucking her hair behind her ear, Sutton said, "Thank Dante. Without the venue, there is no night. In fact, Dante, you're welcome to join us for dinner, if you're free. We're talking logistics and expectations, so..."

"He's free," said Kent, giving Dante a shove.

And Dante found himself wishing that the old

Kent was back; the hunched, disengaged Kent who barely looked him in the eye.

"So, yes?" Sutton pointed to her table.

Dante rounded the bar and followed where she led. Gaze on her hair, reminding him it smelled like peaches and sunshine. The sweep of her shoulders reminding him of how she'd thrown her arms around his neck. The sway of her hips had his fingers curling into his palms.

When they reached the table, he was glad to have something to do with his hands. He pulled out her chair.

"Thanks," she said, her voice breathless. Her gaze flickering between his eyes, then dropping to his mouth, then away, before she all but fell into the chair.

He chose the seat across from her, hoping the distance would give him some reprieve. Only the view of her gathering her hair and twirling it over one shoulder, picking up the menu and pretending to read it, nibbling at the inside of her bottom lip, unspooled more longing, only this time inside him.

Then she rolled her eyes, slammed the menu on the table, flattened her hands atop the thing, and looked at him. "So."

"So," he said, leaning back, crossing his arms.

To which her mouth lifted at one corner. "Where's the purple T-shirt?"

"Early retirement."

"Pity."

"Why is that?"

Swirls of darkest blue washed into her eyes. "Could be good for business. Bring in a whole new kind of clientele."

Dante uncrossed his arms, and let his hands fall to the table, his fingertips landing an inch from hers. The knots unravelling in the face of her warmth, the silent conversation happening beneath their words.

"Any other advice?" he asked, shifting his hands forward an inch.

She noticed, her fingers curling, then uncurling. "Kent should be full-time, and front of house at all times."

"Kent costs almost as much in breakages as he does in wages."

"He's faster on POS than you are. And he's a delight."

"Are you suggesting I am not a delight?"

"Not in the least," she said without pause. "Though I'm not sure he'd look quite as good in purple as you do."

Dante shook his head, slowly, side to side. Then pressed his hands forward so that his fingers slid along hers. Her breath hitched, and she curled her hand so the palm faced upward. Vulnerable, trusting. *Hell.*

"Sutton," he said curling a finger around hers—

"Sorry, I'm late!"

The both of them snapped their hands back as Laila the bookstore owner dragged out a chair and sat at their table.

"Well, this is a turn," said Laila, looking from Dante to Sutton, her eyes widening in obvious question.

Sutton's mouth pursed as she shook her head at the other woman, a silent conversation if ever there was one.

"Hey."

All three looked up to find Niccolo standing over the table, his gaze moving over the women, landing on Laila for a long fraught beat, before he said to Dante, "What do we have here?"

"Nothing that concerns you, Constable Good-boy," said Laila, waving a dismissive hand.

Nico bristled.

And Dante, delighted in the turn of events, said, "Care to join us?"

"The more the merrier!" Sutton added. Before wincing, as if she'd been kicked under the table.

Nico slowly moved around the table and took the fourth chair. Then he looked to Sutton, then Laila, then Sutton—realisation dawning in his eyes.

"The brunette," Nico said, clicking his fingers Sutton's way.

"The younger cousin," Sutton clicked back. Then she held out her hand. "Sutton Mayberry."

Nico took it. "Niccolo Rossi."

"Pleasure." She smiled, wide.

And Dante watched his cousin melt. The urge to do some under-table kicking of his own was strong.

"Shall we order?" Dante asked, sliding menus across the table.

"Then to business," Laila grumbled.

Once they'd chosen their meals, Sutton insisting they all save room for donuts for dessert, Dante suggested wines to match. Sutton ordered a lager. Then shot Dante a quick private shrug that had his insides turning over on themselves.

Nico picked up the handwritten "Reserved" sign and waved it at Dante. "Business must have quadrupled overnight for this to be a thing."

Avoiding Sutton's gaze, Dante took it and slid it into his pocket. "Laila and Sutton are going to host an event at the Vine. A singles night."

Sign forgotten, Nico frowned, his gaze going straight to Laila. "What might that entail?"

"Well," Laila said, batting her lashes and curling a finger in her hair. "I'm thinking we black out the windows, add a few red lights, bring in some chaise lounges, a couple of swing sets, hand out handcuffs at the door—"

"It will be a perfectly sensible and sophisticated evening," Sutton jumped in. "The Vine can turn a nice profit while we help the younger locals make new friends."

"Don't bother," said Laila. "Nothing is wholesome enough for Captain Perfect."

Nico, pretending, badly, that he'd not heard her, said to Sutton, "That's actually not a bad idea."

"Right? It won't take much to zhoosh this place up," Sutton said, reaching into her bag for a notebook and a pencil, then sketched out how they might set the space up.

"We have fairy lights in storage at the villa you can use," said Nico.

Sutton clicked her fingers joyfully in his face.

Laila, shaking off her shock, added, "We could do, say, three signature cocktails for the night— you can charge a packet for those."

"As a first-time thing," said Sutton, "I suggest a soft opening. Adjust the space depending on how many tickets we sell. Learn from it. If it works, it could become a regular thing."

"So, when are we doing this?" Nico asked, tagging himself as a part of the crew.

"How about Saturday week?" said Sutton, glancing at Dante. As if checking if he'd still be in town then.

He nodded. She smiled. And the air crackled.

"I can send out word to my mailing list tonight," Laila jumped in. "I already know a bunch of my regulars, book clubbers, who'll be there like a shot. You know everyone else," she said, half looking at Nico. "Spread the word."

"Team Singles!" Sutton put her hand into the

middle of the table. Nico went next. Laila's hand hovered over his, as if she feared she might get some boy disease before she placed it atop. The three of them looked to Dante.

With a foreign sense of whimsy, he added his hand to the clump, and the others cheered. After which Dante sat back, tucking his hand under his arm, as if it might help keep that feeling a little longer.

Laila brought out her phone and started penning the invitation email, while Nico and Sutton argued over what they should call the event.

"If there is a hint of wine or grapes or vines in a single suggestion," said Laila, thumbs flying over her screen, "I will scream."

Nico opened his mouth. Laila opened hers. Then Nico held up both hands in surrender.

The wine arrived, and Dante offered to pour. He held the bottle close, caught the notes of berry and cashew and spice, all but tasting the scent on the back of his tongue as he let the liquid— a fine red with a translucent rosy hue, a peachy shine—spill gracefully into each full-bottomed wineglass.

When the bottle reached the wineglass in front of Sutton, she slid a quick hand over the top. "Not for me."

"Won't you even try it?" he asked, his voice low.

Sutton's eyes, such a soft sultry blue, looked between his. And the "try it" suddenly felt a lot like "try me."

As if he'd said the words out loud, her tongue darted out to wet between her lips. His gaze dropped, caught on the sheen. Remembering how her mouth had all but brushed his ear, a puff of happy breath scooting across his cheek.

"I don't think it's a good idea," Sutton said, her voice barely above a whisper.

And when he looked up, saw the tumult in her eyes, he knew they were no longer talking about the wine.

"Can't hurt," he said.

"Oh," she said, with a quick sorry smile, "but it can."

Dante watched her a moment, before he nodded, and drew the wine back to his side of the table.

The lager arrived. Sutton smiled at the waiter, took the drink, and drank straight from the bottle. When she ran her finger over her lips, then let out a big sigh, Dante felt at a loss.

Not that she'd not try his wares. It was the loss of possibility. Something he'd not allowed himself to think about in a truly long time. Only now he'd had a taste of it, he wasn't sure how to go back.

After that night, Dante ramped things up—hiring a bookkeeper to tidy up the office and files and internet banking, suggesting Chrissy take on Kent as assistant manager, full-time, and updating Celia in person, by having dinner at the villa most nights.

He'd had to endure a long hug, but Celia had made no mention of mushrooms, or allergies, or Isabella again.

Had he been doing so as it was in the best interests of the Vine? Yes.

Had it also meant he could avoid working the bar floor, thus avoiding a certain customer, one who still had a table reserved every day? Probably.

Not that it made a lick of difference to the direction of his thoughts, anytime they saw a gap.

Can't hurt? Oh, but it can.

The poignancy behind her words haunted him. He knew why he was hesitant, but her story was unknown. Who in her past had hurt her? He wanted names, addresses, almost as much as he wanted to put it out of his head.

All he could do was remind himself that the last thing *she* needed was to get mixed up with the likes of him. Busted, bruised. *More Sasquatch than human*, Nico had called him when he'd landed on their doorstep.

A crash from outside the manager's office, followed by a chorus of voices calling, "Taxi!" snapped him from his reverie. The scent of stale beer and old paper in the office invaded his nostrils with such alacrity, he wondered if it might be damaging his facility for good.

When more raised voices came through the door, he ran both hands over his face, and made his way out into the bar proper.

To find Sutton leaning bodily over the bar. Pressed up onto her toes, loose men's tweed pants hugged her backside, while low on her hips. A fitted T-shirt clung to her in a way that had Dante's mouth turning dry, and a sandal swung lazily from her toes as she lifted a leg to get better purchase on whatever she was reaching for on the other side of the bar.

Dante looked to the gods, begging for forbearance, before he entered the fray. "What was that crash?" he asked.

Sutton's face turned to him, her eyes warming; a smile dashing onto her face, as she shuffled back and her feet dropped to the floor. "Hey! I didn't know you were in."

He kept his smile cool. "The crash?"

"Right. Sorry. I was chatting to the football guys over there, convincing them with great enthusiasm to come to Starry, Starry Singles Night, when I smacked a coffee out of the waiter's hand."

She held up the rag she'd found. And one of the kitchen staff—Dante couldn't remember his name—grabbed it and rushed to clean up the mess.

Dante noted belatedly that the place was busier than usual. Several tables were filled with locals having late lunch, and a few guys in football uniforms had pushed tables together to have post-practice drinks. Nico was up a ladder, being directed by Kent as to where to pin yet more fairy lights.

And Sutton—who'd set up her laptop and papers on the far corner of the bar, near the now half-empty donut cloche—was directing a delivery guy as to where to put boxes of electric candles she'd ordered.

When she turned, face flushed, eyes bright, and skipped over to him, Dante had to press his feet into his shoes so as to keep himself from tipping.

"While I have you," she said, "I've been thinking that it might be fun to build a stage."

Dante leaned against the bar and looked out at how much the space had changed in only a few days. "The event is tomorrow night. I'm not sure even your persuasion skills could make that happen."

"Oh, I could make it happen. I can get a temporary demountable, full lighting, and sound rig organised and set up in two days. But I'm thinking more for the future. This place is solid brick, windows double glazed, you could get a late-night music venue license, no sweat."

When he gave no reaction, certain that if he did, it would give away how impressive he found her, she poked him on the arm. "This place was built for live music, Dante."

"Which will be someone else's problem. When I am long gone."

"Fine," she said, then slunk back to her end of the bar. Where she began tapping furiously at her laptop.

Seeing no coffee at her elbow, Dante moved behind the bar, grabbed an espresso glass, and set to making her a cup. "What are you working on over there?"

When she looked up, her smile told him she'd not been so deeply invested in her work after all. "One of the bands I manage—the Magnolia Blossoms— have been offered a record deal with a reasonably well-known label. I'm working my way through a hundred-odd pages of legalese because chances are there are nasty clauses that will make it harder to say yes than no."

"Might that not be a job for a lawyer?"

"Live and in the flesh," she said, holding out both arms and swinging her torso back and forth, as if presenting herself to him. "I started managing bands for fun while I was in law school. I only take the first pass, then hand it over to a dedicated entertainment lawyer."

"I imagine this band of yours must be seriously good."

"They are spectacular," she gushed. "Finally gaining the notice they deserve, after appearing at Glastonbury last year. Probably time they move to an all-purpose management firm, but were my first band, I was their first manager, and they're stubbornly sticking with me."

"You sound extremely okay with the thought of them leaving you behind."

"Not okay...pragmatic. I'm really good at spotting raw talent, and getting them in front of the audiences who'll love them. The lucky ones will evolve beyond me, requiring hair and makeup teams, PR on retainer. No point getting too attached to something if you know you're going to lose it one day."

She shook her head a little at the last, before getting back to her contract. And while he felt certain there was more going on behind her words than he understood, who was he to pry? He who had walked out on his own family so that people would stop asking if he was okay.

He angled the spoon handle against the inside of the milk jug, and poured a dash of hot milk into the glass. "You sound awfully philosophical."

She shrugged. "I chose a tough industry."

Coffee made the way she liked it, he took it over to her. "You think the music industry is tough, you should try winemaking."

She took the coffee, her finger sliding against his. Dante felt the effect of it far longer than the heat from the glass.

"Please," she said, "from what I saw, 'winemaking' looks to be all wandering through sun-drenched vines and getting tipsy on testing."

"What you *saw*?"

Sutton sipped, paused, swallowed, then said, "So I might have googled your vineyard."

Dante blinked.

Sutton filled the silence. "Sorello. Umbria. You mentioned it that day in your office."

The day she'd thrown herself into his arms.

A few beats slunk by before she said, "I read that you changed its name, when you bought the place a few years back."

Dante wondered what else she'd read. His story would not be hard to find. His family infamous enough for the fallout, and the tragedy behind it, to have made national news. But her expression was merely curious. About him.

"When we were little, my sister…" His heart contracted, as it always did, always would, upon picturing Isabella when they were young. "We would pretend that the southern hillside of the Tuscan vineyard where we grew up belonged to us. We imagined experimenting with varietals, creating genetic wonders that would take the world by storm. We called it Sorello, which, in Italian, means *siblings*."

"Oh," she said. "I love that! It's so…whimsical. Not a word I've imagined relating to your life."

"You've imagined my life?" he asked.

She narrowed her eyes. "I had you pinned as living in some dark castle, all tragic and brooding, frightening local children. Though now, having seen pictures of your place…" She cocked her head. "Dante, it's so beautiful. Honestly. Elysium incarnate."

Dante could not deny how glad he was to hear that's how she felt. "There might yet be skeletons in my attic, you know?"

"Pishposh. Now I'm certain you take in stray kittens, and bake muffins, while your…significant other picks daisies for the kitchen table." She bit back the follow-up question.

And where he'd avoided answering it once before, this time he said, "So close. All bar the significant other."

Her eyelashes fluttered sweetly as a smile flashed across her face. Then she frowned, and looked down at her hands. "Anyway, it's stunning. And the empty hillside leading away from the house—it's the perfect spot for an intimate, day-on-the-green-type music festival."

At that Dante laughed. Rolling pangs of mirth that loosened other feelings in its wake. "Are you ever not on?"

"Hustle, baby. It's what I do."

"Likewise."

Her smile encouraged explanation.

"In between the baking and rescuing of stray kittens—"

"Of course."

"—there is the stress of crop yield, the threat of viruses, of unruly weather patterns, constant battle to find good staff, escalating shipping costs. Then there is the dark-underbelly stories of deliberately damaged barrels, strange accidents, missing bottles. A neighbour of ours woke one morning to find an entire field of vines missing. Torn out overnight."

"You're kidding!"

"I am Italian. We do not kid about wine."

It was her turn to laugh, a gorgeous husky sound that drew glances from tables away. As her laughter faded, her gaze dropped to his shoulder, roved down his arm, all but tracing the tattoo hidden beneath his shirt.

Then she dragged herself back into the moment. Looked at him. And said, "Um, I have to go. Just remembered I'm heading to an art show opening at Corked Creations—a gallery up the road. My dad is a big fan of modern art, so might have visited back then. Though I might be able to drum up a few last-minute Starry, Starry Singles Night ticket sales while there. You?"

"I'll be here, herding monkeys." He gestured to where Kent was holding the bottom of the ladder, admiring the view of Nico above.

Sutton laughed again, then gathered her things. "Then, I guess I'll see you tomorrow. If not tomorrow night, for the big event?"

Dante nodded.

With one last look, tinged with heat, and ques-

tions, and loaded unspoken things, she left. And
Dante breathed out fully for the first time since
he'd seen her by the bar.

CHAPTER FIVE

So much for a soft launch, Sutton thought, watching the line of well-dressed people make their way to the Starry, Starry Single Night registration table at the Vine and Stein's front door.

Once the attendees collected their name tags, and velvet pouches containing takeaway gifts as well as details of some fun games the evening had in store, it was her job to encourage them to head inside, where the place was already pumping.

For the Vine and Stein looked an absolute treat. Nic and Kent had done an amazing job, draping the "sky" with hundreds of fairy lights. The tables had been set up to create spaces to sit, as well as dark corners in which people could chat, leaving the centre of the space a place to mill. To case the crowd. To dance.

The bones really were there—the high ceilings, the gothic architecture—to turn the place into something special. A bit of expense, certainly, and some imagination on part of the owners, but it would be so worth it. Make Vermillion a place not just for those looking for a twee touristy day out, but a destination for wine, beauty, and great music—the holy trinity.

Maybe she'd find a way to meet Nico's mother, plant the seed there. For it wasn't Dante's call. In fact, if this night went well, and the crowds kept improving as they had since she'd first arrived, Dante could soon go home. To his beautiful, halcyon, rural escape, with its golden sunlight, and sweet local village, and his lack of a significant other to pick daisies.

The clock inside her head started to tick double time.

What had she said to him the day before? *No point getting too attached to something you know you're going to lose.* Yep. Good advice. Hang on to that.

"Okay, time for you to go inside," Laila stage-whispered as she hustled past in a sparkling silver catsuit with a deep V and nothing underneath.

The dress Laila had leant Sutton—a.k.a. insisted she wear upon threat of death—felt like something a 1940s movie star would wear to bed. Black, satin, high neck, sleeveless, the fabric shifting over her like a caress, and with a thigh-high split that gaped shockingly every time she took a step. She wondered how soon she could slip out of the heels pinching at her toes and shrug on the Vans she had hiding in a bag in the office.

Sutton checked the others on registration were

good to go, and when one slid into her spot, she slipped inside.

Only to stop on a dime when her heart lodged in her throat.

Dante?

At least she thought it was him. She had to blink to make sure. For in lieu of his usual flannelette shirt and jeans he wore an actual suit. His long hair and scruffy stubble had been trimmed, tamed, making him look less like a bear and more...

The saliva pooling in the back of her mouth made words impossible.

Only he needed to *not* be her focus that night. Things had been so busy, leading up, she'd conveniently let herself forget why she'd agreed to help Laila in the first place. To find a connection to her parents' experience, by opening herself up to meeting someone new.

Maybe someone who liked the kind of music she liked. Someone who liked to travel. A great conversationalist. Someone who made her feel even a fraction of the spark she felt when looking at the man in the suit casing the edges of the room, like he was ready to grab any troublemakers and haul them out by the collar.

Dante, she thought on a sigh. Only *not* Dante. Anyone *but* Dante.

Dante, who listened to Dean Martin records, was a homebody, grunted more than he spoke, and was clearly not open to anything happening between them. Despite the fact that they sparked, and flirted, and somehow found ways to be together more than was necessary.

Time was ticking. It was only a couple of weeks till her birthday; till she was the age her mother was when she'd been given no more chances. This was not the time to prevaricate. Love lightning was a stretch, but this night was opportunity, at the very least.

She gave her dress one last tug, so as to maintain some sense of propriety, then readied herself to meet as many single men as the night allowed. But first she needed a drink.

The fact that Dante had moved behind the bar was by the by.

Sure, a voice in the back of her head scoffed. *You tell yourself that.*

Sutton felt flickers of interest as she moved across the floor, but only peripherally. For her attention was on Dante, who had quickly gathered himself a fan club, a veritable plethora vying for his attention.

"I'm as flabbergasted as you are."

Sutton looked up to find Nico standing beside her. Wearing a suit, no tie, he'd scrubbed up mighty well himself. Yet she felt none of the same visceral turmoil as she did at the sight of Dante.

"Did he get a *haircut*?" Sutton asked.

"Looks that way."

Still long, his hair no longer hid the deep warm

brown of his beautiful eyes, the cut of his cheek-bones, the newly tamed stubble, the hard angles of the jaw beneath.

He leaned forward as one of the singles crooked a finger his way, asking for a drink. Or maybe his phone number. Or firstborn child.

His frown as he leaned back made Sutton's tension ease.

There he is, she thought. *There's Dante.*

And like rocks atop a mountain tipping into an avalanche, heat spread through her, turning her knees to liquid.

"Huh," said Nico.

Sutton looked his way to find him watching her with a small smile on his face. "What?"

"Nothing." Nico lifted both hands in surrender. "Wine? Signature cocktail?"

"Gin gimlet. Lime. No garnish."

Nico grinned. "Coming right up."

As Nico moved behind the bar, half the crowd seemed to roll in his direction. Dante, sensing the shift, looked up, his gaze going straight to her. There it stayed. Caught. Locked onto her for several long, hot moments.

Then, as if coming from a trance, he shook his head, lips pursed into a long silent whistle.

Sutton, feeling the full force of his blatant approval, cocked her head. *Right back at you.*

Something shifted in his eyes; something deep, rich, heady, and unstoppable.

Then someone walked between them; Chrissy, moving the crowd aside so she could ask the Rossi men a question.

Spell broken, Sutton spun away. Hand to her heart, to find it racing, she gave herself a few moments to catch her breath.

"Gimlet on lime. No garnish," Nico said, from behind her, his voice coming to Sutton as if from underwater.

Sutton murmured her thanks, turned long enough to grab the drink, lifted it, drank it in one go, placed the glass on the bar with vigour, then headed out into the throng.

"It's game time!" Laila called over the speakers. "If you haven't already, check your pouch for the name of a famous romantic literary character. Then go forth and find your match."

Sutton opened her velvet pouch to find a slip of paper with a name on it, and laughed out loud.

She'd helped Laila put together the goodies each attendee would receive—a box of chocolate hearts, a small bottle of lube, scented condoms, a little black notebook and pen with Forbidden Fruits branding, a ten-percent-off voucher for Forbidden Fruits, and one half of a famous romantic literary couple.

"Sophia Stanton-Lacy and Charles Rivenhall?" Sutton had asked as she'd snipped the laminated names apart.

Laila had shot her a look that was most unimpressed. "*The Grand Sophy?* By Georgette Heyer?"

Sutton had shrugged and moved on to the next. "Georgie and… Vektal?"

"Are you seriously telling me you've not read *Ice Planet Barbarians*?"

Sutton shrugged. "You're a book girl, I'm a music girl, get over it. Ooh, Edward Cullen and Bella Swan. I know them! I think. Maybe not. Who are they again?"

"Heathen," Laila muttered under her breath.

Now Sutton found herself looking at a piece of paper that read Miss Piggy. "If I'm not looking for Kermit the Frog, I'm giving up now," she muttered.

For while she'd mixed and mingled, and convinced a whole lot of people to check out her bands, there had been no sparks. Much less lightning. But the night was young, and her mind was open, and if a person couldn't find even a flutter of romance on a night like this they might as well not bother with it all.

She looked up, hoping to catch someone's eye so she could compare literary names, and as seemed to be her doom, her gaze instead found Dante.

He was out from behind the bar, leaning against one of the high tables at the edge of the room, talking to a really sweet redhead Sutton had met earlier that night. Dahlia? Dahlia—who was smiling and laughing at something he'd said.

And he looked…if not relaxed, then as if he wasn't having a terrible time. Which, for him, was huge. Or was she reading more into it than was there, because the idea of him coming out of that impressive shell of his with anyone but her made her heart hurt.

"You don't happen to be looking for Rhysand?" a deep voice asked.

Sutton looked up to find a tall, ostensibly handsome man with thick sandy hair, perfect teeth, and a dimple smiling down at her. "Sorry?"

He looked at a piece of paper. "Rhysand. I hope I'm pronouncing that right."

When she blinked up at him, he reached for her hand, turned it gently over, and found *Miss Piggy* written on her piece of paper. He laughed. Then leaned in, not too much, but enough to make it clear he was happy to remain right where he was. "Is it wrong to admit I've not recognised a single literary name I've heard thus far?"

Sutton, having finally collected herself, said, "I think he's some kind of fairy? But I'm honestly as clueless as you are."

"Shall we call it even?"

After a beat in which she pictured Dante, smiling and talking to a really nice woman, who was not her, which he was absolutely within his rights to do, she held out her hand.

"I'm Sutton."

* * *

It was nearing midnight and the sky was soft and sparkling. Main Street, Vermillion, with its fairy-light-bedecked avenue of trees, and warmly lit shop fronts, was built for a night like this.

Sutton grabbed the folding table by the front door and took it inside, leaving Nico to look after the last of the stragglers. He seemed to have it under control—taking his job of marshalling everyone onto the footpath as they waited for the courtesy bus, or taxis, or lifts home terribly seriously.

Inside the Vine, the lights of the bar were on low. Chairs scraped through the sticky confetti covering the floor as the staff upended them onto tables, leaving room for the cleanup crew they'd hired to come in the predawn to put the place back to rights.

"Wondered where you'd got to."

Sutton's overwrought nerves sparked merrily at hearing Dante's voice, despite the workload they'd carried all night.

"Just cleaning up, as much as I can," she said, turning to find his hands resting in the pockets of his suit pants, doing things to the shape of him that had her mind reeling.

He'd lost his jacket. His pale button-down shirt was slimmer fit than usual, meaning it pulled just so against his broad chest, hinting at the impressive shape beneath. The slight shadow of his tattoo could be seen through the fabric, curling up and over his shoulder.

Thankfully Dante missed her hungry gaze as his was on the dance floor.

Kent and Chrissy slow danced, a good metre apart, and as if they were on the moon, while "Creep" crooned moodily from the sound system. While Laila was holding a couple of kitchen staff hostage, telling them about some spicy fantasy book they had to read, if their slack-jawed attention was anything to go by.

"How was your night?" he asked, his voice low, rough, as if he'd used his daily allocation of words.

"Tiring," said Sutton. "Mostly."

"Hmm," Dante seemed to agree. Then, "I thought that was your thing—packed bars, loud music, happy people."

"It is. It's just, I'm not usually—" She stopped, not quite sure how to word it.

"The one on show?"

She'd been going to say *I'm not usually one to compare*. But all night that was all she'd done; comparing the dashing ginger-haired gent with the expansive indie music knowledge, and the charming guy who'd been her Kermit the Frog, or any number of others she'd found herself paired with in Laila's litany of games, with the man beside her now.

Glancing up she found Dante watching her,

with that warm dark inscrutable gaze. The jaw beneath his trimmed stubble such a perfect sweep from ear to chin she felt an urge to trace it with her touch.

"Something like that," she managed. "How about you? Nice night?"

"It was, surprisingly." A smile hovering on those beautifully shaped lips.

Sutton's belly tightened. But she said, "I'm glad."

They were shoulder to shoulder, but not touching. There was more than enough physical distance between them to feel perfectly civilised, yet Sutton's skin felt aflame, the urge to lean into him so strong she had to press her toes into her shoes. Hard.

Then she made the mistake of breathing in through her nose. Even after a long night in the bar, he smelled amazing. Like clean skin, and freshly washed cotton sheets, and some rich earthy something that was purely him.

Some fresh ache began to build inside her. It felt a lot like disappointment. As if she'd actually held out some small hope that she'd look across the crowded room and *boom*! The way it had happened for her parents.

Only she'd never had a chance, and it was entirely her fault. She'd spent the entire night wondering where Dante was, what he was doing, whom he was talking to. Because somehow, she'd become stuck on *this* guy. This big, elusive, closed-off, grouch of a man.

What an unholy waste.

"Sutton! Dante! Get the hell over here!"

As one they looked over to find Kent waving while the wait crew, kitchen staff, and temp bar staff had now all spilled into the big empty space, joining Kent and Chrissy in their slow-mo dance.

Prepared to wave them away, Sutton baulked when Dante's hand appeared in her vision.

"You're kidding," she said, looking up to find him smiling down at her. Smiling! Her poor foolish heart. "You *dance*?"

"I'm Italian, we do not kid about dancing." His eyebrows waggled, and the joy that spilled through her was something else.

"Come on!" Chrissy shouted.

"Okay, then." Sutton placed her hand in Dante's, and when his longer fingers closed around hers, it felt so lovely, so true.

Without hesitation, he strode out onto the makeshift dance floor and she had no choice but to follow.

The crowd quickly moved in around them. Then someone started a slow-motion conga line. Rather than joining in, Dante pulled her gently into his hold, one hand holding hers, the other warm and sure on her lower back. And together they swayed.

"Creep" finished, "Unchained Melody" began,

Norah Jones's voice a plaintive sigh echoing through the space. Someone dimmed the lights to a flicker of starlight and little more, and a conga line dispersed into a moonscape slow dance once more.

Dante curled his hand around hers, spun her out to the end of his arm and back again.

She let out a huff of laughter, her hair falling about her face, as her hand landed on his chest. He curled his around it, holding it there. His other arm sliding farther around her back until they were as close as two people could be without public indecency.

Then he breathed out a long-suffering sigh, as his gaze dropped, landing on her mouth. Watching as if waiting to see what she might say next. Or wondering what she might taste like. For real.

Her fingers curled tighter around his and his gaze lifted. Pure smoke, not a hint of a smile. And her heart began to beat double time.

Dante shook his head. A lament. A curse she understood far too well, but had neither the experience nor the courage to break. She wished she could just lift up onto her toes and press her lips to his. She wanted it more than she wanted to breathe.

Instead, she turned her head away, leaned her cheek against his chest. The steady beat of his heart made her feel like crying.

When they turned, a gentle move, the music guiding them, Sutton saw Laila now sitting on one end of the bar.

Sutton lifted her head, mouthed, *You okay?*

Laila lifted her shoulders, gave them a happy wiggle, then grinned as she raised her drink in salute. Then mouthed, *Are you okay?*

Sutton opened her mouth, closed it, and shrugged.

Dante, feeling it, pulled her closer still. Till she felt as safe and secure as if she was wrapped in the world's most luxurious blanket.

Then "Lickety Split" by the Magnolia Blossoms rent the air, all cacophonous vocals and mad drums. And Sutton's head snapped up.

It was enough for Dante to lose his rhythm. The both of them coming to from whatever place had made them think they could dance so close, and get away with it.

"I love these guys!" Kent shouted, grabbing the remote and turning it up.

"They're mine," Sutton shouted back.

"Yours?" Kent asked.

"The Magnolia Blossoms. I manage them."

"Get out of here!" Kent gawped.

Sutton gawped back, spinning in Dante's arms. Only he gently pulled her back against his chest as his hand rested around her waist. She felt the heat of him all over her now. Evidence that she wasn't the only one existing in this strange place between reality and desire, pressed against her backside.

It was so wild, so overt, she laughed, and hiccupped. Then she couldn't stop.

"Who else?" asked Kent.

"Currently?" *Hiccup.* "The Sweety Pies. Candy Carter… I managed Crochet for a bit, before they took off."

Kent glared at Sutton. "If you tell me you've met the Floss Babies, I will literally throw myself off the nearest bridge."

Hiccup. "Does an ironic B&B crawl holiday through the Cotswolds one spring count?"

Kent threw his hands in the air in mock disgust, before grabbing the hands of those nearest and jumping up and down till the floor shook.

Sutton spun back into Dante's arms. And at the sight of his beautiful face, her hiccups just went away.

This, she thought, *this is the very best part of the night.* And that was okay.

"What do you think?" she asked, motioning to the music blasting around them. "They're amazing, right?"

Dante smiled as he shook his head. As if he knew as much about folk punk as she did about wine. Which felt just about right.

Sutton took him by the hand, encouraging him to twirl her out to the end of his arm, only this time she let him go. She laughed at the indulgent

look on his face. Her laugh turned into something
bigger. Freer. And below a canopy of pretend stars,
her favourite band filling the night with music,
Sutton finally kicked off her shoes and danced.

CHAPTER SIX

SUTTON SAT IN the jewel-green velvet couch in the front window of Forbidden Fruits as Laila brought over two glasses and a bottle of Vermillion Hill bubbly.

She held it up and Sutton shook her head no, cradling the coffee she'd picked up from the bakery, as the Vine wasn't open for another hour. The coffee was too milky, and not hot enough, but she hoped it might still work some magic. After very few hours of restless, dream-filled sleep, she needed it.

"You do realise Nico Rossi had something to do with the making of that wine," Sutton niggled as Laila poured herself a glass.

Laila shrugged as she sat in a gilt chair with pink velvet seat. "What that man doesn't know won't kill me. Now, let's break down how last night went."

"A success?"

Laila lifted her bubbly in salute. "Okay, now that's done, did you have fun?"

"I really did." What she didn't say was that the after-party was her favourite part, a million times over. "How do you think everyone else has come up this morning?"

"Not my problem," said Laila.

While by "everyone" Sutton actually meant Dante. It was a Sunday. Would he be at the Vine? She had work to catch up on. Should she head in, reclaim her table? Would things be strange between them, after their dance? If they *weren't* strange, would she be disappointed?

"Now," said Laila, cutting into her reverie, "we have to follow up ASAP with the results from the compatibility tests."

Laila grabbed her tablet from the coffee table and swiped madly over the screen, no doubt bringing up the app she'd sent to all attendees when they bought their tickets, requesting they fill it in. Questions included whether a person preferred bubble baths or showerheads with alternating spray options, so Sutton had limited hopes regards its veracity.

"Anyone in particular you want me to check against your profile?" Laila asked.

Dante's face was the first, and only, that popped into her mind. She blinked it away. "I met lots of nice people, but—"

"No love lightning?" Laila guessed.

Sutton *had* been about to blurt that she'd been having second, third, and fourth thoughts about a certain Grumpy Bartender after holding his hand had felt like a literal highlight of her pretty darned fabulous life.

Then a frown creased Laila's face. "Huh."

"What's wrong?"

Laila looked up, face pure guile. "Nothing. Not a thing."

Sutton clicked her fingers Laila's way. With a grimace, Laila turned her tablet around to show Sutton's profile beside...

"Dante?" Heck, even saying his name now made her feel weak all over. "When did *he* fill out the questionnaire?"

"He was my guinea pig. I made him fill it out a few days ago to check that it worked."

Saving questions as to how on earth Laila convinced Dante to say whether he preferred snuggling up with his special someone beneath a blanket by a fireplace in winter, or skinny-dipping together in a pool at the height of summer, Sutton asked, more than a little breathlessly, "Are you telling me Dante and I...*matched*?"

"Um..." said Laila, as she scrolled down the screen to where *Eight percent compatibility* glared back at them in unhappy, tomato red.

"Eight percent," she muttered. *Eight percent!* Yes, she'd just been thinking it was probably a load of bunkum, but even so, eight percent was pretty damning.

"Ignore it," said Laila. "It was a silly idea. Just

one more way to keep customers on the hook."
Then, "Unless… Were you hoping you had matched
with Dante?"

Sutton opened her mouth. Then closed it. What
to say? No? Yes? Gods, yes, pretty please, with
sugar on top?

Laila put a hand on her knee. "Whatever you are
thinking, stop. You look like you're about to burst
a vein! You like him, he likes you. That much is
obvious to everyone."

"Who's everyone?"

Laila waved a hush-up hand between them.
"The thing is though, in my experience, sexual
chemistry isn't everything. In fact, it can blind
you to the important stuff."

Trying her best to get past the fact that "everyone" thought she and Dante had "sexual chemistry," Sutton asked, "Which is?"

"Location, ethics, lifestyle, family, hopes and
dreams, whether you're a *Star Wars* or *Star Trek*
fan? Who knows? I spend my days surrounded by
men who aren't even human, or real. I'm clearly
not the one to ask."

Sutton made a sound that sounded like a laugh
but felt like a choke. And Laila's smile was far
too understanding for comfort.

"Okay," Laila said, "considering the eight percent, let's count Dante out, for now, and see if
there are any guys with whom you did match. In

case there is someone perfect for you who you didn't get the chance to meet last night."

Count Dante out. Wasn't that what she'd been telling herself to do from day one. Some instinct assuring her she wasn't up for the likes of him. The quiz might be made up, but what if it was also a sign from the universe that holding hands with Dante, dreaming of Dante, dancing with Dante was setting her up for a huge fall.

"Sure," Sutton said, curling her feelings for the man deep down inside her, tucking them into a safe little box where they would hopefully stay this time. "Why not?"

She'd travelled halfway across the world looking for *something.*

The best thing she could do for herself was to keep trying to find it, till she figured out just what it was.

Dante crouched before a Chardonnay and Pinot Blanc hybrid vine, running his hands over the graft, tracing the petals of small white buds flowering at the tips.

It was the first time he'd stepped foot among the vines since arriving in Vermillion. Helping Zia Celia with real estate concerns he could handle, helping Rossi family wines had been an absolute no. Meaning Celia had saved telling him about their new graft until he was primed. Distracted. In a good mood.

That morning, even after very little in the way of restorative sleep, he'd woken feeling invigorated. Enlivened. As if the colours of the world had changed overnight. The need to walk among the vines, any vines, had been impossible to resist.

His phone buzzed. He considered ignoring it—the cleanup crew would have done their job, the staff would all arrive on time; he was sure of it in a way he'd not imagined he could be when he'd first arrived.

But his sense of duty had him wiping the dirt from his hands, before answering. *"Pronto?"*

"Dante? It's Sutton."

"Sutton," he said. His heart slammed into his throat and he stood so quickly he felt lightheaded. They'd shared numbers in preparation for the singles night, but she'd never called him before. "What is wrong?"

"Wrong? Nothing." Then, after a pause, "Took some time to come down after last night, but other than that, I'm great. You?"

Dante, realising he was pacing, stopped and gripped the back of his neck, pressing into the tension that had strangled him the moment his imagination had run away from him. "I slept fine. Thank you."

Though it had been well after three by the time he'd made it back to his bed, for he'd stayed after everyone else had left. To count the night's takings, to restock the bar, to lock up. To think, to reset, reassess.

For while the entire night had been a study in what passion and purpose could accomplish in a wildly short amount of time, the after-party had been something else entirely. Specifically, the dance, with Sutton.

It had lasted less than half a song, yet he'd walked out onto the dance floor with rigid purpose, and left it feeling as if his foundations had been whipped away.

"Where are you?" Sutton asked.

"Vermillion Hill," he said, his voice gruff, throat clutching around all the things he felt he wanted to say to her, but could not. *Should not. Should he?* "You?"

"At the Vine. I thought you might be here."

"I gave myself the day off."

"Totally fair." A beat, then, "You should see the place, though, Dante. There is not a table spare. Even the barstools are full. And there's a line at the door. There are a number of familiar faces from last night—city folk who stayed over, locals, and tourists swept up in the crowd. Chrissy found a lectern and she's set up a booking station at the front door. It's madness!"

Dante blinked into the middle distance. "You are serious."

"As a heart attack." Sutton laughed, the sound

turning up the sunshine. "But that's not why I was calling."

Dante's focus contracted like the crack of a whip as every sense went on high alert. Sutton had *called* him. Sutton who had melted against his chest, her hand playing with his hair, before looking up at him as if it was taking everything in her not to lift onto her toes and kiss him.

"So, this might sound out of left field," she said, stopping to clear her throat. "And if you're not up for it I totally understand."

Dante's heart thundered against his ribs at the possibilities of what she might say. None of which was:

"So, you know the compatibility test?"

"The—?"

"The questionnaire, on the app, that Laila forced us all to fill out."

Ah. Dante could hardly remember how Laila had convinced him to do so. Witchcraft was not outside the realm of possibility. But what did that have to do with the dance?

Then Sutton went on. "Turns out I got quite a few hits. With men. With whom I might be compatible." She went on quickly. "And while it really was a silly quiz, I kind of feel as if I have to let it play out. What if it's the reason I came here? I don't know. Either way, I plan to set up as many dates as I can in the next couple of weeks. And since I don't know these guys, I thought it best to do so someplace safe. The Vine is my safe place. And it would be great to know there was someone, a kind of wingman, on my side, to move them on if needs be."

Dante, who had finally caught up with how the conversation had turned, knew what was coming before she even said the words.

"I was hoping that you might be that person. For me?"

The desire to laugh, and throw his phone across the field, came at him in equal measure. Instead, he pressed finger and thumb to his temple and rubbed.

"I could ask someone else," she said, when he said nothing, "if it feels weird. It is weird right? In fact, I'll try Kent. Or Nico. Though what with the winery and his volunteer work he might not have the time—"

"I'll do it," Dante growled.

She needed him, he'd be there, it was that simple. No matter how deep the cut.

A beat, then, "Thank you, Dante. Just…thank you."

Sutton's hands were shaking as she hung up the phone. She threw the thing on her bed and lay back on the feather-soft mattress with a thud.

Looking up at the lacy canopy, she let out a great big sigh. Then a growl. Then, grabbing a pillow to put over her face, a yell.

For a second there, longer, a deep soul-clutching breath, she'd considered saying something else entirely. Considered telling him how lovely it had been dancing with him. Asking if it had felt special to him too.

But then she'd pictured her dad, sitting in his wing chair every night, listening to her mother's favourite records, glass of wine in hand, heartbroken even today, and such words had felt impossible.

Yes, she wanted to be braver when it came to affairs of the heart. Wanted to open herself up to all of life's big moves before her twenty-eighth birthday. But she wanted to be careful, to ease her way in. And Dante Rossi was anything but easy.

"Good decision," she said to the ceiling.

Then again, and again, until she started to almost believe it.

A couple of nights later, Sutton stood outside the Vine and Stein, her hand reaching for the door, then pulling away. Reaching, and falling back. It felt like her first day all over again, only this time she knew what she was walking into.

"What are you doing?" Laila asked.

"Prevaricating."

"We went through this. You are to get in there early, choose the spot with the best lighting, have a schooner to loosen up, and prepare to fall madly in love. Right?"

"Right." Sutton had agreed to all of it, in theory. "Is this really a smart move?"

"I'm not sure about smart, but it's worth a shot. Now go, get in there. Message me as soon as you're done."

"You're not coming in?"

"Yikes no. You already have one too many people watching over you, in my opinion. You do not need a whole audience. Go get 'em!"

Laila backed away, while Sutton opened the door.

Remembering the chill wind that had rushed through her all those weeks ago, as if a sign that change was coming, she told herself that change didn't always happen *to* a person, sometimes it happened because a person decided it was time.

Five minutes later Sutton sat at her usual table, deciding on comfort over "best lighting."

Someone had set it with a linen tablecloth, and an old Chianti bottle with a real lit candle inside, while Dean Martin crooned from a speaker hidden somewhere nearby. Meaning either "someone" had kindly looked up "classic romantic first date" decor, or they were messing with her.

That "someone" had to be Dante. Dean Martin? And no one else bar Laila knew her plan.

Though the man hadn't even looked up once since she'd arrived. He seemed to be going through paperwork behind the bar, which he could be doing in the office. Meaning he was doing as she asked, and looking out for her, as requested. Right? Not being there, all gorgeous, and grumpy and—

"Sutton?"

Sutton flinched, then looked up to find a man standing by her table.

When she said nothing, he scratched his chest. "I'm Mando. From singles night."

"Mando!" She pushed back her chair, the thing catching on a knot in the wood floor as she stood, so that she nearly chopped herself in half against the edge of the table.

Mando laughed. A nice deep laugh. That was a good thing. Right? A good start?

Once she extricated herself from the table, she took his hand and he pulled her in to lay a kiss on her cheek. He smelled nice. He was good-looking. Yet as he sat in the proffered chair across from her, the urge to look past him, to the man at the bar, was so strong it took physical effort to keep her gaze where it ought to be.

She looked to… Mando? Mando. With an encouraging smile. "So, singles club. What a night, right?"

Sutton had been right about one thing—the Vine was getting busier every single shift. If it kept going this way, they might break even that week.

While Dante should be feeling over the moon, by the third night of their blind date deal, he wished he was hitting a boxing bag at the gym, or chopping down a tree, for he had a sudden surfeit of energy he could not deplete.

He glanced up at Sutton's table, where that night she was chatting with a giant of a man with curly blond hair. Night before had been a dark-haired guy with a ponytail. Night before that a ginger-haired guy with dimples.

"Is that one of Sutton's bands playing over the sound system?" said Laila, who had snuck in after the bookshop closed.

"It is," Dante said.

The first night, once her date had left, Sutton had stalked up to the bar, all riled up as if he'd done something wrong. He who had danced with her, held her in his arms, begun to believe that maybe there was something between them that could no longer be denied, then been asked to be her *assistant* on a series of blind dates.

She'd clicked her fingers at him when he'd not deigned look up the moment she appeared.

"Something I can help you with?" he'd drawled.

"Whatever device is playing the music next to my table—give it to me."

He placed down his pen and looked into her eyes. "And I thought you were a music lover."

The way her lashes had batted against her cheek, the way her tongue had slipped over her bottom lip before she'd dragged it into her mouth… He felt it like a living thing, roiling inside him.

She'd said, "Dean Martin singing 'Memories Are Made of This' over and over again for an hour and a half is not 'music.'"

Dante pulled out his phone, typed in his passcode, and handed it over. "Was your date a success at least?"

"It was fine," she gritted out as she swiped through his playlist.

"As far as I know the Vine has never hosted a wedding reception, but we are all about trying new things here now."

Her eyes were sharp, her smile fake, as she handed back her phone. "Great. I'll keep it in mind." With a dark look, she'd grabbed her stuff and left.

Not five minutes later she'd texted him an apology for being so abrupt, thanked him for his help, signed off with Sutton x and made him feel like a bad friend. And like more than a friend as he took that *X* and imagined meanings that were simply not there.

"Ooh, I remember this one," said Laila, dragging Dante back into the present to find Laila watching Sutton and her date laugh together. "Hot. Big muscles."

Dante grabbed a bar towel and wrapped it tight around his hand till his fingertips turned numb.

Nico—who had been sitting at the other end of the bar, pretending to ignore Laila—sauntered to sit at the seat beside hers, and said, "She's smiling. That has to be a good sign."

"It's not reaching her eyes," said Dante, as he wiped down the bench hard enough to take off a layer of shellac. "Not the way it does when she really smiles."

After a pregnant pause, Laila and Nico spun on their barstools to stare at him.

"Not a word," Dante growled, as he stalked into the office. "Not a single word."

After a late-afternoon tour of a local historical house, Sutton hustled up Main Street, on her way to her next date with a guy named… Greg? Or was it Craig? After a week of blind dates, they were starting to blur.

At least she knew if it was worth extending the dates past a single drink quickly now. The night prior she'd given Dante the signal, shaking a hand through her hair, to let him know to come to the table with a "phone call" after less than ten minutes.

Her phone rang with a real call as she neared the Vine. When she saw it was her dad, her heart leaped into her throat.

They'd been in touch—sending funny cat memes, and checking in with their daily Wordle scores. She'd called a couple of times too. Sure, she'd known he'd be at work, but she'd left long messages, asking after his shifts at the local grocery store.

But it had been long enough. The time had come to tell him the truth. Spotting a bench beneath a cheery blossom, she sat, and picked up the call.

"Dad!"

"Honeybun! I'm so glad I caught you. You've been busy?"

"Good busy."

"Glad to hear it. You know I've been hoping it's because you've met someone nice."

She laughed, as was expected, only for the first time in her life she wished she could tell him that she had. "I meet nice people every day, Dad. You know that. Now how about you? Booked that Devon walking holiday yet? The scenery looks gorgeous. All that fresh air. Did you show Marjorie?"

A pause, then, "It sure looked wonderful, honeybun."

Sutton bit her lip as even she could hear she was being far pushier than usual. But the fact he spent his nights alone, when he was still young enough to carve out a different life, it pained her.

When her dad made no further comment, she braced herself and said, "So I have some fun news. You won't believe where I am right now."

"Where's that?"

"Sitting on a bench on the Main Street of Vermillion." The silence that met her was heavy. Heavy enough she said, "Dad? Are you still there?"

"By Vermillion you mean…?"

"South Australia. Where you met Mum!"

A strangled noise came from the other end of the line.

Heart in her throat, Sutton shifted to the edge of the seat. "Dad, are you okay?"

"But why?" he said. "Why would you do that? Why would you not tell me you were going, so I could… I could…"

Sutton held her tongue. The same protective instinct that had stopped her from telling him where she was, was now telling her to give him grace.

"So you could tell me your favourite haunts?" she allowed. "I would love that, actually. I keep wondering if I've visited the same places you guys did."

When he said nothing, she put the back of her hand over her eyes. "I've upset you, haven't I? This is why I didn't want to tell you. But it's a *nice* thing, Dad. I'm twenty-eight in a few days, the same age Mum was when she died. And coming here felt like something I had to do."

"Of course," he said, after another long silence. "Of course, my love."

"Are you sure?"

"Its fine, honey," he said. "I understand. Enjoy yourself, and when you come home, tell me all about it."

"Okay. Love you, Dad."

"Love you, honey."

Sutton rang off. Then sat there for goodness knew how long, cradling her phone, and feeling more confused than ever.

Sutton looked miserably into her drink. It was her third. Or fourth. She'd needed something to distract her from the conversation with her dad.

Her sweet, loving dad who'd been nothing but wonderful to her. She'd not wanted to hurt his feelings, and now she was all but certain she had. Yet there was more going on, something behind his reaction, she was sure of it.

And instead of finding out what that was, she was on a stupid date. With a stranger. Because she was too much of a scaredy-cat to ask out the one person who actually floated her boat.

"Sutton?"

Sutton looked up to find Craig, or Greg, sitting across the table, looking at her with concern. She lifted her hand straight up in the air.

His gaze followed the move. "Are you okay?"

"Yep, just signalling my wingman so he can come rescue me."

"Your… *Seriously?*"

Realising she's just said that out loud, she winced. "It's not you, it's me."

Greg, who was gathering his things, said, "Yeah, you've got that right." He grabbed his glass of wine—a delightfully plummy Vermillion Hill red he'd spent their entire date orgasming over—downed the dregs, then left.

Sutton slowly slid down deep in her chair. Footsteps neared, then stopped. She lifted her head to find Dante standing by her table. "Oh, hi."

He glanced at her arm, which was still raised in the air.

Sutton dropped her hand and patted the seat beside hers. "Sit."

"I'm working."

"No, you're not. You've done all you came here to do. Now you're just pretending to work so that you can stay here and spend time with your family who you miss terribly. You're all just too stubborn to admit it."

Dante's jaw worked. Yet, for whatever reason, he sat. "I think you need some water."

"Water-schmater. And wine-schmine for that matter." She flicked her date's wineglass a *ting*. "What's so good about it anyway? A grape is a grape is a grape."

Dante, mouth twitching, said, "I have offered to show you why that is simply not true. But you have refused me. More than once."

She looked at him, sensing a hidden message between his words too. Men and their secrets! *Pfft.*

"Fine," she said. "Show me now."

Dante shook his head. "Not now."

"Why?"

"Because I'm not sure you'd remember it afterward."

Sutton swallowed, certain she was missing something now. Certain her lucid self would kick her for not knowing what it was. So instead, she frowned down at her cocktail, the colour lost to the silvery sheen of melting ice.

"Are you okay?" Dante asked.

"I'm not sure that I am." When she looked up, her beautiful grumpy bartender was watching her with a level of tenderness she did not know how to deal with.

"Tell me something in Italian," she blurted.

Dante, seeing her change of subject for the distraction that it was, leaned back in his chair, and looked at her from under his dark brows. "Such as?"

She leaned forward, and reached across the table. "Anything you like. Let that ridiculously sexy voice of yours go for broke."

After a long, loaded beat, in which she saw Dante's pulse leap in his throat, the man crossed impressive arms over his impressive chest and said, *"Cos'è rosso e si muove su e giù?"*

"Hmm?" was about as eloquent a response as she could come up with, for she was only half paying attention to his words. That face, those eyes, his body language were all so damned compelling it was hard to think of anything else.

A smile kicking up the corner of his mouth, he added, *"Un pomodoro in un ascensore."*

"But what does it mean?" she asked.

"It means," said Dante, "what's red and moves up and down?"

Chrissy, who was passing by with a drink order, said, "A tomato in an elevator."

"Si, bene."

Dante smiled, Chrissy smiled, Sutton frowned.

Then, expression turning serious, Dante said, "Chrissy, I'm going to take Sutton home."

"Nice," she said with a grin.

Dante's smile disappeared. "Not like that. She's...under the weather."

"Oh. Right. You go, we've got this. Take your girl home."

"Home?" Sutton called after her. "I have no home!"

"The B&B," Dante offered gently, now standing by her chair, holding out a hand. "What was it called? Grape Expectations?"

"If you say so," Sutton said, then, with only a moment's hesitation, put her hand in Dante's, wondering why it had taken her so long to do just that.

Sutton leaned her head against Dante's car window, her breath creating small patches of fog on the glass. Dante wondered if she'd fallen asleep.

If so, what ought he do once they arrived at the

B&B? Rouse her? Walk her to her room? Carry her? The thought of having her warm body tucked up against his chest again, her head tucked under his chin, her hands wrapped trustingly about his neck again, was enough for him to grip the steering wheel hard.

"Sutton," he said, when they turned up the pretty driveway leading to the B&B.

"Hmm?" she said, her voice forlorn.

"We're here."

"Here," she repeated. "My mum and dad fell in love *here*, did you know that?"

"I did know that."

"And I can't even meet someone who'll stick around longer than one drink. What's wrong with me?"

Not a damn thing, he thought as he bumped up the driveway and pulled into a visitor spot in front of a three-story inn.

He turned to face her. "You are discerning."

"I'm broken," she said. And a single tear slid slowly down her cheek.

Dante cut the car engine, so that the only sounds were the tick-tick-tick of cooling metal, the haunting calls of night birds outside, and the myriad thoughts spiralling through his head.

He was the broken one. Sutton was vitality personified. The more he knew her, the more he believed that she was light, and life and... She needed to talk to someone, this was clear. In that moment, busted or not, he was all she had.

He turned more fully on the seat, his knee an inch from hers.

"You're not broken, Sutton," he said. "At least no more than the rest of us. But something has clearly happened to upset you tonight."

Sutton tipped her head to face him, more tears pooling against her lower lashes. "I was a maniac back there. I should have postponed the date. Or cut myself off. Instead, I made that poor man sit with me and bear the brunt of my self-immolation."

She closed her eyes and sank deeper into the seat. "I can't keep going like this. Living in the moment, going with the flow, sleeping where I land, or one day I'll wake up and I'll be sixty and alone and unable to see a way out."

"How old are you?"

"Twenty-eight next week."

"So not quite sixty, just yet."

She sniffed, a smile kicking at the corner of her mouth before disappearing again.

"Meaning," Dante went on, "you have a little time to sort yourself out." Then, well aware he was talking to himself now as much as he was to her, "If you admit to your own foibles and limits, as well as the things you truly want, only then do you have the chance to improve your situation. Right now, here, think of this as a good start."

"I guess that makes sense," she said, then after

looking at him for a few long beats, she curled herself to face him. Her gaze roving over his cheek, his jaw, his neck, before moving back to his mouth. Where it stayed. While she sighed a hearty sigh.

Dante's gaze took in her determined chin, her shoulders lifting as she sniffed, collecting herself. Before being inexorably drawn to her mouth too. To the slide of her tongue over her lower lip, the catch of it between her teeth.

Before he felt himself move, Dante reached up, his fingers cupping her jaw, his thumb tugging at her lip, setting it free.

Her breath hitched, and she swallowed hard. Before her lips pursed, and kissed the end of his thumb.

Gaze fogging, desire swarming over him, Dante ran his thumb over her lip again. The soft, plump give was like everything he'd imagined it to be, and so much more.

When she leaned in, her teeth scraping over the end of his thumb, he felt so many feelings at once he feared he might expire on the spot.

Then, remembering how many drinks she'd had, he gently curled his hand away. When her eyes lifted to his, confused, he smiled, not wanting her to feel she'd done a single thing wrong.

Then her eyes looked past him out the car window. And she screamed.

Dante spun to find a tall thin balding man in a cardigan and tiny glasses barrelling toward them.

"Sutton," the man called, his voice muffled by the glass, "is that you?"

Dante opened the car window. "Barry?" He'd called the man before coming, hoping he'd have a spare key to Sutton's room.

Barry leaned into Dante's window. "Dante, I assume? And how is my little pepper pot?"

"Rubbish," Sutton said. "Sorry I screamed."

Barry waved it off. "Happens more than you'd think. I have snacks. A bucket of water for you to drink. Your bed is turned down for the night."

"Thank you." She gave Barry a huge, grateful smile.

Then turned that smile on Dante. His heart twisted in such a way he wasn't sure it would ever be right again. "Thank you for being my wingman."

"Anytime."

A million thoughts seem to scurry across her eyes. She opened her mouth as if about to say something, then snapped it shut. With one more tight-lipped smile, she hopped out of the car.

Dante waited till she was in the front door, Barry bouncing around protectively behind her, before he gunned the engine and drove away.

CHAPTER SEVEN

THERE WAS ONLY one other car in the staff parking lot when Sutton pressed the buzzer at the back door of the Vine and Stein—the Range Rover Dante had driven her to the B&B in over twenty-four hours before.

She'd woken twelve hours later feeling sober and sobered by the choices she had made.

Forcing herself to go on blind dates? That wasn't her. Not telling her father her plan before she left? That hadn't been sensitive, or fair. As for Dante, and the walls she kept building between them, when all he'd done was be generous and supportive the entire time?

It was now three days till her twenty-eighth birthday and the near constant *tick-tock, tick-tock* in the back of her head had clearly sent her around the bend.

There were so many sensible reasons why leaning into her feelings for Dante wasn't the savvy thing to do. Yet, there was no escaping the fact that from the moment she'd first set eyes on him, felt that restrained bear energy, she'd honestly *liked* the guy. The very least she could do was make it clear to him he wasn't merely her wingman, chauffeur, or barista. She was truly grateful he was in her life.

She lifted her hand to knock again when she heard footsteps behind the door. It wasn't a cool night, yet an anticipatory shiver rocked through her. And when the door opened, Dante on the other side, the light of the single bulb over the back door making him look as beastly as ever all she felt was relief.

"Hey," she said.

"Hey." He leaned in the doorway. "How are you feeling?"

"Fine," she said, then, "better. Thank you." Then, "Can I come in?"

Dante hesitated; hesitation being his prime mode of communication where she was concerned. The both of them as bad as each other.

"Let me in, Dante."

After a hard breath out, he opened the door wider. She slipped through her gap, the brush of her arm against his chest sending shivers of awareness through her.

Door shut behind them, he led her via the kitchen, into the bar. Only the emergency lights, and the desk lamp in the office, were on.

The look of the place was reminiscent of that first morning, but every other thing about it was

significantly different. She now knew this man—
more than he probably wanted, and less than she'd
like. And the energy that crackled between them
as he turned to face her was filled with a history
of days, weeks of building tension.

"So," she said, hitching her backpack, "I came
here tonight to thank you for—"

"No need."

"Let me finish, please."

He held out both hands. "Of course."

"Thank you for driving me. I honestly can't
remember if I said so last night, so thank you."
Noting a mark on the bar, she rubbed at it with
her thumb as she said, "On top of that I want to
apologise for putting you in that position in the
first place."

When she looked up, Dante had his arms
crossed. Barriers up, yet watching intently, listening fully, as always.

"You've been so generous, letting me work
here, allowing us to take over the place for an
event that was a complete Hail Mary, not rolling
your eyes every time I sprout some idea on how
you could improve the Vine—"

"Sutton," Dante said, his voice low, quiet in the
semidarkness, but carrying to her all the same.

"Not finished," she said, unable to meet his
eyes for this last part. "Asking you to watch over
me while I met other men, when you and I... I
mean, I don't know what we are. To each other.

But we're enough of a something, I think, that asking that of you was a crummy thing to do."

Her heart was thudding so hard by that point her ears rang. Yet she forced her gaze to his as she said, "Okay, now you can talk."

Dante's dark gaze was impossible to read.

"Did I blow it?" she asked. "Tell me what I need to do to make you like me again."

"Sutton," he said, voice pained. He took a step forward, then stopped. *Always* stopping.

While she'd lived by the mantra of throwing herself at every opportunity life put in her way, in every part of her life bar this one. She let her backpack fall to the floor with a slump. Then took a step toward him. And another. And another.

Dante's chest rose and fell, but he did not move.

One more step and the tips of her Vans kissed the tips of his boots. Then she lifted her hands and laid them against his jaw. "Talk to me," she said. "Please."

His stubble was softer than expected against her palm. She ran her thumbs over the skin above his stubble and could feel him vibrating. She looked up into eyes that were dark pools of swirling smoke and said, "If you want me to leave, I will. If you want me to stay, I will. I'm sick of questioning myself where you're concerned. Tell me what you want instead."

Her hands slid away from his face, and dropped to his chest. Beneath her touch, his heart was as erratic as her own. It was enough for her to curl her hands into the cotton of his shirt and give him a frustrated little yank.

He went with it, swaying to her as if she had control of him, of his breath, his body, his next move.

So, she did it again. Pulling him closer, only this time not allowing him to sway away.

Then a sound came out of him, like something that had been kept locked away for centuries, and his arms swept around her, lifting her off her feet, as his mouth came down on hers.

And oh, it was a kiss that had been a long time coming. Building. Hovering on the edges of their interactions until they were stupid from wanting.

After a few long moments, in which time felt suspended, his lips began to move over hers. Hot and slow, the bristles of his stubble tickling at her skin. His arms slid farther around her, holding her as close as he was able.

The emotion that swelled inside her as this man held her was like nothing she'd ever felt. Gentle and wild, soft and deep all at once. When he found a way to hold her tighter still, she moaned against his mouth.

With a growl, he deepened the kiss. Sweeping his tongue into her mouth, as if she was his breath, his very life force. The pressure sending her backward, till she bumped against the bar. It was so glorious, she huffed out a puff of laughter, of pure joy.

It was enough for Dante to snap back into his body—she felt it happen. He pulled back, flinching away from her, as if he'd been shocked.

She grabbed at him, hauling him back, wrapping a leg around his calf so he couldn't get away. And he didn't, not yet. But neither did he kiss her again. Breathing hard, he let his forehead drop to hers. And swore, softly, in his native language, while the hand at her waist gripped her, as if he was loath to let her go.

"I tried so hard not to let that happen," he said.

"Tell me about it," Sutton said on another huff of laughter.

He slowly shook his head, his hair catching on hers. "I had good reason. Without it I'd have given in to this, to you, weeks ago."

"Are you sure about that?" she asked, having recently pulled her own "reasons" apart as easily as dandelion fluff.

He lifted his head. Her heart hitched at the hardness of his gaze. "I am sure," he said. "Even now. I cannot give you what you need, *tesoro*."

Something inside her threatened to crack. But she braved up and said, "I think I know what I need better than you do."

Dante lifted his hand to cup her jaw, thumb tracing her cheekbone, the edge of her brow, the movement so sweet, so tender, especially when contrasted against his next words. "I am not the man you think I am."

"And what kind of man do you think I think you are?"

"A man who can treat you with casual regard and live with himself."

Sutton winced. For this moment, this man, had felt anything but casual. Not that she could tell him so; her bravery only went so far.

"Then you know what you can do?" she said, with what she hoped was a sassy smile. "Treat me with thorough regard, instead."

He laughed, a deep rumbling sound that all but took her knees out from under her. Then, eyes almost black with desire, he placed a finger under her chin and lifted her face, pulled her close, and kissed her.

A kiss so gentle, and so sweet, he might as well have yanked her heart off its leash. Leaving her unprepared when Dante pulled away again.

The hand at her side gone, the man moving away so that she could not reach for him again, she had to grip the edge of the bar so as not to collapse in a molten heap.

"Dante?"

"Scusata," he said, shooting her a look that made her heart tremble. "I'm sorry. I can't. I just… Do you need me to drop you home?"

Sutton blinked. Barely able to remember where

she was, much less how she'd got there. "I... I drove."

He nodded. "Then I will see you out."

"I...sure. If that's what you want?"

A beat later, so many emotions washing over his face she had no hope of keeping up, he said, "It is."

She reached down for her bag, lifted it listlessly onto her shoulder, and led him back through the kitchen and out the back door.

He waited for her to get safely to her car, before he lifted his hand in a wave, and closed himself inside the Vine.

Sutton coughed out a laugh, though there was no humour in it at all. "Good. Great," she said to the empty night. "Glad we cleared that up!"

A flicker of lamplight through the frosted glass of the back door told her Dante was at the door, pacing. That she wasn't the only one left feeling askew.

When the kitchen light switched off, with a loud, Dante-esque growl, Sutton gunned the engine and left.

"Happy birthday!" Laila sang, as she leaped out at Sutton as she trudged through the foyer of the Grape Escape on her way back from breakfast.

Sutton, still in her pyjamas, found herself holding a bunch of helium balloons with a mix of baby paraphernalia and Disney characters on them.

"It's all they had left at late notice," Laila apologised. "Anyway, go get changed, I have a day planned."

Sutton looked longingly up the stairs. She was finally twenty-eight. Her plan had been to mope under the blanket in her room and let this day of all days pass her by with a whimper. Especially after the disaster with Dante the other night. All her impetus to explore the town, connect with her parents, open herself up to lovey-dovey stuff had felt flat after that. Enough she'd even begun thinking maybe it was time to leave.

Laila turned her around and shoved her toward the stairs. "I'm taking you somewhere fabulous. A Vermillion must-see. You'll love it, I promise!"

"Okay," said Sutton, shaking off the doldrums and deciding what the heck. Birthday spirit, it was. "Dress code?"

"You do you, Boo. Just make it quick. Because... yep! Our bus is here."

"Bus?"

Laila pointed through the front window to where a small bus, filled with a dozen or so other people, awaited them. Vermillion Hill Cellar Door Tours written in bold red font on the side.

Sutton stood at the back of the small tour group, listening with half an ear as the guide talked about the history of the vineyard. Delighting as she was in the gorgeous old stone buildings, trees growing up against their rooves, the cobbled paths with horse and cart tracks worn into grooves over a century before, and the gentle hill covered in squat grey grape vines rising up to what the tour guide called "the family house."

"Are the Rossi family in residence today?" Laila asked.

"I believe so," the tour guide said, solemnly. "We see them on occasion. You might be lucky today!"

Laila nudged Sutton in the ribs. "Hear that? You might get lucky with a Rossi on your birthday!"

Sutton, who had *not* told Laila about the events of the other night, coughed, choked on the cough, and was given first entry into the cellar door space, so she could grab a glass of water before the tasting.

The cellar door was tiny, smaller even than Sutton's B&B room. No windows, ancient grey stone walls, uneven slate floors, massive wood beams crisscrossing overhead.

Behind a rustic wooden counter stood a man in his early twenties, neatly trimmed facial hair, red flannelette shirt over dark jeans. "Hey, I'm Josh. I'll be hosting your tasting today. First time at Vermillion Hill?"

"We're Vermillion Hill virgins," said Laila. "And it's this one's birthday!"

Josh's smile never faltered. "Happy birthday.

How this works—I'll pour a taste of each of the six wines on the menu, you drink, and hopefully we can find you a new favourite drop."

He passed each of them a list of the wines they were set to try, a mix of red, white, and fortified vintages, awards and plaudits attached. He then set up a pair of fresh wineglasses, and spoke of organic certification, biodynamic systems, malolactic fermentation as he poured. While Sutton's gaze kept straying to the open doorway in case a certain Rossi might stride past.

"Nice legs," said Laila, swirling her glass dramatically, before downing the lot in one go.

Sutton spun, saw Josh leaning over to put a bottle away, and pinched Laila on the arm. She whispered, "You can't say that!"

"Legs is the lay term for the grip and drip of the wine as it slips down the inside of the glass."

Warmth slipped down *her* insides as Sutton spun to find Dante strolling through the door. Backlit by golden sunshine, he was all broad shoulders and sexily mussed hair, and the longing that rose in her was overwhelming.

"It speaks to the viscosity of the blend," Dante continued as he moved in beside her, easy as you please, and motioned for Josh to lay out a third glass, "but has no relation to the quality. Yes?"

Josh smiled. "Quite right."

Sutton looked to Laila, asking all the questions with her eyes.

Laila batted her lashes innocently, then leaned back to catch Dante's eye. "Hey, Dante, fancy meeting you here. Do you know Josh?"

Dante held out a hand to the man behind the counter. "Josh. Dante Rossi."

"Signor Rossi, it's an honour," Josh fawned. "Are you happy for us to follow the menu, or would you prefer to choose for our guests?"

Dante waved a hand, as if just happy to be there. The man who famously never looked happy to be anywhere.

"Next up, the Red Velvet," said Josh, holding up a bottle. "We grow many varietals here at Vermillion Hill—Riesling, Semillon, Chardonnay, Grenache. But the Barossa is best known for Shiraz."

Once the wine was poured, Dante picked up his glass using the stem, held it at eye level, and swirled it in a way that made the liquid swish up the sides of the glass without tipping over the edge. He lifted the glass to his nose, breathed deep, then sipped. Eyes closed, strong throat working, expression solemn.

Sutton wanted to kiss him, right there, where his throat bobbed. She bit her lip to stop herself from whimpering at the effort of not doing so.

After placing the glass on the bench, Dante turned to her, expression quizzical, then looked at her hand, which was gripping the bowl of her delicate glass with all her might.

He laughed through his nose, the smile hitting his eyes, and her heart quickened. What was happening right now? Where was the usual grouchy Dante mask? It usually did a pretty good job of hiding his thoughts, but now she could see pleasure in his gaze. Pleasure that flowed through *her* like a waterfall.

Leaning in, voice low, he said, "The point of a wine tasting is to taste the wine."

"Told you," Sutton managed to say, "I'm not a wine drinker." Her father was the wine drinker. Every night, listening to those records, as if the sense memory might bring him back to this place.

"Then why are you here?"

"Laila's idea."

Laila and Josh chatted nearby, voices muted, as if they'd moved to the other end of the small bar to give Sutton and Dante some privacy. If he thought that was her doing…

"I didn't come here, in the hopes of—"

"I know," he said, eyes crinkling. "I know."

Then his eyes dropped to her mouth, as he slowly breathed out, and the memory of their kiss, the way he'd held her as if she was something precious but also something he wanted to ravish with every fibre of his being, made her body hum.

Yes, he'd put a stop to it, which had shaken her. But while it had felt like a rejection, he'd actually rejected *himself* on her behalf. And she'd never know why if she hid from him, or kept pushing him away.

She swallowed, and said, "A while back you said you thought you could change my mind."

Dante cocked his head.

"About wine."

"Ah."

"I'm willing to try now, if you are."

Dante's gaze was potent. Focused. Then with a nod he looked to Josh, at the row of wines on a shelf behind his head, and said, "Is there a San-giovese Grosso 2003 Vigna dell'Essenza near-about?"

Josh's eyes widened, then he disappeared through a small door, footsteps leading down to what must have been an underground cellar, and came back a couple of minutes later with an older-looking bottle. Sutton recognised the sketch on the label as the house from the large photograph on the wall of the Vine and Stein office.

Only once Dante nodded did Josh slip the cork free with a soft pop. He sourced two fresh glasses, and poured a very small amount into each.

This time Dante simply drank the proffered wine and the sound that came from him—throaty, appreciative—traced Sutton's spine like a slow, deliberate finger. When he looked to her, she had to press her knees back hard so as to keep them from giving way.

"Do *I* just drink?" she asked. "Or ought I do the whole swirl, sniff, sip thing?"

"Just drink," Dante said.

Hands trembling a little, for it was clear this wasn't just any bottle of wine, Sutton lifted the glass to her mouth, took a swig, and swallowed it down.

"Then tell me what you think," said Dante.

"It's…strong," she said, on a little cough. "Spicy." The aftertaste kept changing depending on which part of her mouth she focused on.

"Good," he said. "Now try it again."

He nodded and Josh poured for them both again.

Dante dismissed him with a polite movement of his head before turning to Sutton. "Only this time, swirl the glass like this, to let oxygen play its part. Then close your eyes, let the scent fill your nose. Then take another sip, and allow *all* your senses to take part. Wine is not a drink so much as it is a sensory experience. A memory, a tradition, a connection to the earth, the sky, the past."

Sutton, feeling as if she was about to take a test for a subject she'd not studied, went through Dante's instructions, one by one, finally allowing the wine to coat her tongue, the sides of her teeth, the back of her throat.

Dante's voice crooned, "The Sangiovese is a grape well known to Siena. High acid, vibrant, fresh. A grip that softens with age. The Vigna dell'Essenza brings flavours of dark cheery, leather, spice. It was a dry year, low rainfall, resulting in a complex, full-bodied vintage."

Sutton had always thought the language surrounding wine sounded so unapologetically pretentious. With Dante weaving a story in her mind as the liquid moved over her taste buds, she felt a ripening, sensed latent sweetness, imagined electric storms with no rain.

"How do you know so much about a single bottle?"

"As children Nico and I, and my sister, Isabella, helped pick the crop you are enjoying now."

Sutton slowly opened her eyes to find Dante watching her. His expression serious. She swallowed again, and as the wine hit her belly, it seemed to catch on the thread of heat she could see in his eyes.

"What do you think?" Dante asked.

"It...tastes like grape?"

Dante blinked, his eyes moving to the bottle, to her glass, to her face, then he burst into laughter. A rough, raw, sound so deep and inviting she felt a heated smile warm her face.

Then his hand landed on her back—a warm, solid touch that had her wanting to lean into him. To turn and bury her face in his neck. And wrap her arms around him and climb into his arms and not let go.

It also made her wish they'd never met.

For try as she might, she could not see this ending the way her relationships usually did. Like a crew at the end of a fun tour—hug, shake hands, and move on. Despite all the effort she'd put into not letting her crush on the guy move beyond that, she'd already failed.

Then Dante raised his glass to her. "Happy birthday, Sutton," he said.

She lifted hers, clinked, then they took their final sips together.

Josh cleared his throat and said, "What would you like me to do with the bottle?"

"Enjoy it," Dante said, not taking his eyes from hers.

"Seriously? Thank you."

"No time like the present," said Laila.

"It's a thousand-dollar bottle of wine," Josh murmured.

"Then earn your keep, Joshy-boy. Convince me this thing is as good as those two made it look."

Sutton, feeling a little as if she wasn't entirely in her own body anymore, said, "I think I need some air."

She put down the glass, turned, and all but bolted outside, where she found a bench seat carved from a fallen tree. She sat; fingers curled around the wood, sun dappling her skin through the branches of a tree swaying overhead.

She wasn't surprised when Dante sat beside her.

Out of the corner of her eye she saw him lean back, arms crossed, legs stretched out before him. In the sunshine she noticed his jeans were old, boots scuffed, skin was swarthier than usual—all signs he'd been working at the vineyard all day.

He breathed out a long slow breath, as if he felt...*at ease*. Something she had never seen at the Vine. There he was all clenched jaw, hard eyes, a constant growl beneath his words. Here, under a wide-open sky, the scent of dirt and flowers in the air, near the thing that gave him purpose, it hit her that she was seeing Dante, in his natural environment, for the first time.

While grumpy Dante tied her in knots, this Dante might just be her undoing.

Giving up on finding her feet anytime soon, she slid down in the seat, crossed her arms, crossed her feet at the ankle, and let her head fall back against the back of the bench.

They stayed like that for several long moments, before Dante said, "Tastes like grape." Then he laughed again.

And this time Sutton laughed with him.

"I'm so sorry," she said, covering her face, before looking at him through one eye. "I like grapes, if that helps."

He laughed again; this time his gaze stayed on her. Then, with a hard outshot of breath, he said, "You've not been around the past few days."

"No," she agreed.

"Might that have something to do with the other night?"

She looked up at the tree swaying overhead. She *could* talk about it—she wasn't afraid of tough conversations, unless they involved her dad, clearly. She just didn't want to hear Dante tell her he liked her, only not that way. Not the way her father had seen her mother and just known. Not today.

"It's my birthday," she said. "That means I get to decide what we talk about and what we don't."

"Fair," he said, then pulled himself upright. "So, what would you like to talk about?"

"The weather? It's a pretty nice day for a birthday."

"So it is," he said, not taking his eyes off her.

She pulled herself upright as well, taking the chance to put an inch of space between them. Only when her hand landed on the bench, her little finger brushed his. A moment later his hand moved over hers. Warm, rough, steady.

"There you are!" Laila cried as she burst out of the cellar door, as the next group went inside for their turn.

Sutton gently moved her hand to her lap.

"What did I miss?" Laila asked. "What were you guys talking about?"

"My birthday."

"On that," said Dante, pressing himself to standing, "if you're free, how does lunch at the villa and a proper tour of the place sound?"

When Sutton looked to him, he raised a single eyebrow in what looked very much like a dare. Who was this man and what had he done with Dante? Then it hit her—maybe it wasn't simply the location. What if by fronting up, grabbing the guy by the shirt and kissing him, she had changed things between them after all?

"Sounds fabulous to me," said Laila, checking her bag for her sunglasses, before moving in to give Sutton a one-armed hug. "You two have fun."

"You're most welcome to join us," Dante said.

"And if you're leaving, I'll come with you," said Sutton.

"Stay," said Laila. "I'll go talk Joshy into another glass of that spectacular wine, then go back on the bus with the others. I have plenty of boxes of books to unpack, anyway. Better now than late tonight," Laila said. She pointed a finger at Dante. "Make sure she gets home safe."

"Will do."

"Happy birthday, my love!" Laila called, then disappeared back into the cellar door.

"Shall we?" Dante asked, holding out a hand.

Sutton, wondering how the universe had put her there again, took it.

CHAPTER EIGHT

WHEN THEY REACHED the eastern vineyard of Vermillion Hill, Dante stepped into the field only to find Sutton had stopped short.

"Are you sure I can go in there?"

"Why would you not?"

"It feels like a sacred space. Out of bounds. What if I have one of those diseases on my shoes the tour guide was talking about, or a bug on my clothes. What if I poison them with my perilous lack of wine knowledge?" Then she whispered, "What if they know?"

He placed a hand at her back and gave her a light push, enjoying having her there beside him more than he'd have ever imagined. The soft quiet of the vineyard, so different from the dark, the noise of the Vine, along with the sunshine and dust motes, made time stretch out before him.

Soon Sutton walked ahead, turning back to ask questions every now and then—about the crop, or the process, or what it was like back home—or simply running a hand over the vine leaves once assured it was okay to do so.

While Dante spent every second in between remembering how it had felt to hold her, to pull her close, to kiss her. How hard it had been to let her go.

In the moment it felt like the right thing to do.

It wasn't as if he'd denied himself pleasure in his life. Or companionship. He ate well, drank well, had work that gave him immense satisfaction. It was just that it already felt like far more than he deserved. For if Isabella was unable to enjoy such an abundance of delights, why on earth should he?

Sutton Mayberry was, quite simply, more than he could ever accept. Her vitality, her bumptiousness, her...*amore per la vita*, the way she gathered people close, and threw herself at life with such abandon.

He'd spent weeks telling himself she was not his to want.

Now, watching her stroll his family's land, in the hazy stillness of a warm afternoon, he felt his self-denial slipping. For how could being with her, laughing with her, watching her enjoy the world be wrong?

It was a slippery slope. One that would take vigilance, if he was to get out of this place without doing something for which he'd truly never forgive himself.

She stopped at the edge of the vineyard, where a single-lane dirt track cut up the hill toward the house. "Question."

Bring it, he thought.

"The vines on that side of the path," she said, pointing to the left, then pointing to the right, "and these—why are they so different?"

Dante moved up beside her, his skin twitching from how near she was. And gave her a lesson on the differences between the thick, squat, twisted, Grenache bush vines and the daintier, trellised Pinot Noir. Which led him to tell her about his Sagrantino vines back home.

"Comparatively, the leaves of the Sagrantino are a vibrant orange this time of year—the local hills look like fire in the autumn light. Come winter, the vines are bare. Spring hits, the buds appear, new wines are released. We pick in summer. And it starts all over again."

He looked to her when he was done to find her smiling up at him. Hands on hips, cheeks pink from exercise.

"Look at you," she said, "all puffed up and proud. You're practically giddy."

"I am not giddy."

"You are so giddy," she said, moving to knock her shoulder against his. "We are lucky, you and I. To do something we feel passionate about. Not everyone finds that in life."

On that they were in agreement.

He motioned they head up toward the house.

"How does this place compare to Sorello?" she asked, falling into step beside him,

"Land-wise, Vermillion Hill is probably three times bigger. We would be considered a boutique label in comparison. But the latitude and climate are similar."

"Do you miss it?" Sutton asked.

"Enormously," he admitted. "But I have a good team running the place in my absence. We check in once, twice daily. All, I am assured, is well."

"I'm sure they'll be glad to see you return. Soon."

He felt the question hovering between them: *When might that be?* The Vine was much improved, only he could not seem to pull the pin just yet.

"How about you?" he asked. "Are you missing home?"

"I tour a lot, so I don't really have a place that feels like home. Not in the way you do." She swallowed. "Though my dad and I are very close. Only we argued, the other day, just before my disastrous final blind date, which we never do."

"Have you spoken to him since?"

"We've messaged, but no. No calls. And no mention of the argument. He'll call me later today, for my birthday, no doubt. Maybe I'll bring it up then. Maybe not." She shook her head. "You've mentioned a sister. Is she in the family business too?"

They were near enough the house, he knew

he could change the subject easily enough. Only with her looking up at him, her genuine interest in what made him *him* clear as day, he found himself saying, "Isabella passed away quite a number of years ago."

Sutton stopped. Reached for his arm when he kept walking. "Dante? What happened? Or... Don't tell me, if you don't want to."

He took the hand on his arm and tucked it into his side once more, forcing her to continue walking toward the house. "She was several years younger than me, making her terribly young when our mother died. My father made it clear he preferred me. He found me easier, I think. She was bright, creative, completely uninterested in the family business. They knocked heads, constantly."

"That must have been hard," said Sutton, sliding her hand a little farther up the side of his arm so that their bodies brushed as they walked.

"Hmm. We were close, so that gave her some protection. Only as she hit her teens, and their relationship became more combative, she fell in with friends who were not good for her. It was around the same time that I was becoming more involved with Rossi Vignaioli Internazionali, firstborn son, bred to take over one day. It got to the point where she wouldn't even talk to me."

Step, brush, a gentle squeeze of his arm. It kept him tethered, even as his mind went to events he'd done as much as possible to distance himself from. Fearful that if he ever leaned into them again, this time he might never lean out.

"One night, I had planned to be home for dinner, but having spent all day trialling a new fermentation process on a small batch of grapes I had grown on my own, I was late. All we can figure is that she had been drinking, went for a swim in the southern dam…" He swallowed. "I found her late the next day, unaware she'd even been missing."

Sutton tugged so hard on his arm then, he had no choice but to stop. Then she turned him so that he faced her. Her spare hand slid up to his shoulder, then when he refused to meet her eyes, she cradled his cheek, lifting his face so he had no choice.

"I'm so sorry. The way you spoke of her, of your plans when you were younger, I had no idea."

"Of course you didn't. I never talk of her," he admitted.

"Why?" Then, with a frown, "Don't tell me you think it is *your* fault."

Dante shook his head. He *had*. But over time he'd come to see the cogs and spokes and moments that had led to what was a horrific accident. "My father did not feel the same, unable to see his part in her self-destruction. When he began telling everyone in the family what I had, and had not done, to help, I could not take it anymore."

Sutton's eyes blazed in fury. Then she moved

her hand, as if about to run it through his hair, in comfort. In care. Only at the last second, she stopped herself. Brow furrowing as if she remembered what had happened the last time she'd touched him.

When she made to take her hand away, Dante's hand caught hers, and after a pause, slowly placed it back against his cheek.

Her eyes grew dark. Her chest rose and fell. Then her thumb traced a slow arc over his cheek. The hand still curled around his arm pulled him close and she leaned her cheek against his chest and held him. Pure comfort, and kindness—her way of showing him that she was on his side.

Then her phone rang, and he felt her flinch against him.

"I'm so sorry," she said, slowly uncurling herself from around him. "That's my dad's ringtone. He'll be calling to wish me happy birthday."

"Answer it," he insisted, bringing the hand that had been at his cheek to his lips so that he might kiss her palm. Then he let her go.

Looking as if emotion and sense were warring inside her, she stepped back, and answered. Her voice sweet and kind, as she said, "Dad, hey."

Dante moved a little farther way, giving her privacy as she paced back and forth. He heard the occasional *mmm-hmm*, and *thank you*, and *love you, Dad*. The rest he only picked up by way of her body language.

Something wasn't right. Most people wouldn't see it, but he did. He recognised in her a need to wear a mask at times, to keep people at arm's length. While his was cantankerous, hers was a show of strength.

And it hit him, for all the ways they were dissimilar—beer versus wine, travel versus home, preference for noise versus quiet—in the deepest, most personal ways, they might actually be very much the same.

When she hung up the phone, she shot him a quick smile, the slight wobble making a protective instinct rise up like a roar inside him.

"You okay?"

"Sure. He'd love to have seen me today, of all days."

"Is it tradition to spend your birthdays together?"

"It's not that. It's just… My mother died when she was twenty-eight. Today I'm twenty-eight. He adored my mother. When she died it all but destroyed him. It's a big part of why I came here."

Dante wished he could give her the solace she had just given him, but she was coursing with an excess of energy, where in such moments he tended to shut down.

She shook her head, and pocketed her phone. "I'm probably making something out of nothing. Either way, I've taken up enough of your day. I should probably let you be."

"Stay," said Dante before he felt the word leave his mouth. "Please."

Her gaze moved over his as she made her decision. He did not blame her for taking her time. Until now he'd done his utmost to find reasons not to spend time with her. A kiss had changed it all. Changed him. Now he was flying without a map.

"Stay," he said, moving in, cupping her elbows, "have lunch with me. A birthday celebration. My aunt Celia will be there. Chances are Niccolo will join us, which will give you the chance to watch him be taken down by his mother."

"Bonus," she said, leaning into his touch. He wasn't sure she even knew she was doing so.

"Is that a yes?"

She looked out over the vineyard, then down to her phone, then with a smile that would forever more be burned onto the backs of his retinas, she said, "That's a yes."

Where the cellar door was quaint, the private grounds of Vermillion Hill were pure elegance. A sweeping stone home perched atop the hill, tennis court, indoor pool, wings seemingly added over the years. All of which Sutton would have gushed over, if her mind wasn't still so snagged on her father's call.

Unlike the last time they'd spoken—when he'd stuttered, and seemed not himself—not only had he informed her he'd looked into the walking tour, he had asked Marjorie, the neighbour, to come over with her laptop so they could look at more pictures online together.

Which was good. Great, even. Only the timing felt too fortuitous to be a coincidence.

"Sutton! What a delight!"

Sutton turned to find Nico walking toward them, wearing what looked like a firefighter uniform. "Ah, what's happening?" she muttered to Dante.

Dante leaned in, murmuring, "My cousin likes playing hero in his spare time."

Sutton thought to the way he tried to keep Laila in line. "Only in his spare time?"

Dante's laugh shifted against her hair.

"Hey, Nico," she said as he neared. "You didn't have to dress up for my birthday. Unless… Oh, my gosh, are you a strip-o-gram? If so, go ahead."

Nico blushed. Blushed! Glared at Dante, then leaned in for a double-cheek kiss. "Happy birthday, Sutton."

When he moved back, Sutton felt Dante move in closer. Proprietarily.

"What are your plans?" Nico asked.

"Dante asked me to stay for lunch."

Nico looked over Sutton's shoulder. "Did he, now?"

"He did," said Dante, his voice deep with warning.

"So long as that's all right with your mother," Sutton added.

"Are you kidding?" Walking backward toward the door of the house, a dimpled grin on his handsome face, Nico said, "Wait till my mother gets a load of you."

Sutton had never found cause to use the word *insouciant* till she met Celia Rossi.

Niccolo's mother—a.k.a. Dante's aunt, who had begged and pleaded and guilted him into coming over to "save the Vine"—was the epitome of casual elegance.

Celia whipped her large sunglasses from her face as she went first to Dante. *"Caro!"* she intoned, drawing her nephew in for a double-cheek kiss.

Nico, looking most put out, said, "Firstborn son, here."

His mother tutted, before pulling him into her embrace. "You get plenty of hugs. This one has been in deficit for far too long."

She patted Dante's cheek, then her gaze swung in a wild double take as she saw Sutton. "What have we here?"

"Zia," said Dante, *"questa è* Sutton Mayberry. She co-hosted the recent singles night at the Vine that was such a success. Sutton, my aunt Celia Rossi."

Celia's eyes narrowed in a way that had Sutton wanting to tug at the waistline of her low-slung jeans and put on pearls. "Are you the bookstore owner giving my Niccolo such troubles?"

Sutton smiled. "I'm the tourist who found herself swept up in the bookstore owner's madcap, but ultimately successful, plan."

Celia, clearly appreciating the light sting in the tail of Sutton's words, held out a hand. "Then I am very pleased to meet you, Sutton. You are staying for lunch, no?"

"Yes? If that's all right with you."

Celia slid a hand through Sutton's arm and led her toward the house proper.

"It's Sutton's birthday," Dante warned. "So be nice."

"*Buon compleanno.* And shush, I am always nice."

Sutton let out a sigh as she leaned back in the plush outdoor chair, having enjoyed an astonishing assortment of cheeses, cured meats, olive oil, and breads over the past few hours. For lunch had come late, morphing into early dinner, and while Celia flitted in and out, Dante and Nico had chatted, laughed, and told stories of their childhood together.

She'd even made her way through a half glass of wine—too scared to offend Celia to say no.

Did it taste like grape? Yes.

Would she try some again, off her own bat? Undecided.

Considering the long lead-in to this day, and the deep reverence she'd attached to it, it had turned out pretty darned wonderfully. Much of that thanks to the man sitting across the table, watching her in a way that had her feeling as if her blood was filled with bubbles.

Nico grabbed the closest bottle, filled a glass for himself. Dante shook his head, done. While Sutton had to wave him away again, even after she'd done so several times. They were wine pushers, the lot of them.

"Tell me about yourself, *mia cara*," said Celia as she settled into a chair, curling her feet up, glass of wine in hand. "What is your story?"

Having told more people "her story" than she'd ever imagined she might over the past few weeks, Sutton gave Celia the CliffsNotes, touching briefly on why this birthday was bittersweet. Concluding with, "I wonder if you ever met my father. Gerard Mayberry? He was a backpacker, working around here when I was born."

"Alas, we've only been here the past twenty-some years. The children were primary school-aged when Rossi Vignaioli Internazionali bought the Vermillion Hill estate. Yes?"

Nico nodded.

"Was it your choice to move so far away?" Sutton asked, feeling a pang at living permanently far away from her dad.

"A little distance from family is never a bad

thing," said Nico, as if parroting a line he'd heard many times before.

Dante's, "Mmm-hmm," had Sutton turning her head, in time to watch the movement of his throat as he swallowed a mouthful of wine. She remembered the graze of that stubble on her own skin, the way those lips felt on hers—

"And your mother?" Celia asked. "Was she from around here?"

Dante's gaze rocked to hers, his big body curling forward on his seat, as if readying to swat the question back if need be. Sutton shook her head, and he backed down.

"They met here," Sutton said, "lived here for a while. But she passed away when I was young."

"Ah. I am sorry to hear that." Then, "Her name?"

"Mya. Mya Hawthorn."

Celia blinked. And turned to her son. "Nico, *ho sentito bene*? *Ha appena detto* Mya Hawthorn?"

Nico, who had been only half paying attention, looked to Sutton and said, "Mya Hawthorn was your mother?"

Sutton nodded. And swallowed, hard. Her gaze flicking between Celia and Nico. For something in both of their expressions had lifted the hairs on the back of her neck.

Then Celia smiled and said, "What a lovely name! Now, Dante, tell me, how are you and that little pub of mine getting on?"

And the hook in Sutton's belly let go.

"The Vine is a changed place. The staff have stepped up, taking ownership, coming up with new ideas to keep it in the public eye, in order to help it stay that way."

"Well, that's nice."

"Nice?" Dante repeated, after a beat. "I came all this way as you assured me the entire Vermillion Hill business would be on the verge of collapse if I did not."

"Well," Celia said, lifting her wineglass between the tips of her fingers, "I may have exaggerated."

Sutton looked from Dante, to Nico, then to Celia.

Holding out her glass for a refill, which Nico promptly afforded her, Celia added, "It has been a loss leader for a decade, now. We've had offers to sell, but we feared the new owners might stock it with non-Rossi wine, so we kept it. I may yet knock it down and build rentable shop fronts."

"No!" said Sutton, imagining the Vine crumbling. All that potential going to waste.

Thankfully, at the same time Dante, chastised, *"Zia!"*

"Do not *Zia* me, *ragazzo*. I am an old woman. The benefit of which is that I may say and do as I please. Including inventing a reason to bring you out here, in the hopes of shaking you out of your silly doldrums."

Sutton grabbed a piece of capsicum and nibbled, in order to stop herself from calling out again. Considering the storm clouds gathering over Dante's head, she wondered just how much of the thorn in his paw had to do with his family situation. Quite a bit, she guessed.

"La mia stasi era tutt'altro che scioccaas," Dante shot back, no doubt explaining that his doldrums were anything but silly.

"*Si.* But everything, good and bad, has its time. Your banishment, self or otherwise, should never have gone on as long as it did. It's time we all let that go."

"Let that go," Dante growled, sounding very much the Dante of old. "By that do you mean I am to let Isabella go?"

Celia's fraught gaze slid to Sutton, who paused mid-chew.

"She knows about Isabella," Dante said.

And his aunt flinched. *"Caro,"* she said, "I was speaking of my brother-in-law. Your father. His challenges. His choices. It is time we each stop letting that shape our lives, now that he is long gone."

Dane's nostrils flared, before he let his head fall into his hands.

Nico muttered, *"Mamma Mia,"* under his breath, as if he'd heard it all before.

Celia held up both her hands in surrender. "*Scusa.* Everything I do I do in love." Then, turning to Sutton, reaching out and taking her hand.

"Forgive us for making such a row on your birthday. We are an emotional family."

"Nothing to forgive," said Sutton, "when everything you do you do in love."

At that Nico snorted. Then began to laugh. So loudly he rocked back in his chair and held a hand to his belly. Soon Dante's shoulders were shaking, his own laughter close behind.

Celia's smile was slower, as she took in her nephew with wide eyes. When Dante lifted his head and looked to Sutton, smiling as he shook his head, Celia's gaze moved on Sutton once more. This time it stayed, as if seeing her for the first time.

Sutton didn't realise the older woman was still holding her hand until she felt the grateful squeeze.

As Dante led Sutton out to the Land Rover, she shivered, for night had fallen fast. It tended to, when his family got to talking. He didn't realise how much he missed the rubbish, the ribbing, the reminiscing, till that night.

"Are you cold?" he asked.

"A little."

Dante took his jacket from his back, and draped it over her shoulders. She instantly slid her arms into the sleeves with a low hum of appreciation that he knew he'd be replaying in his head for some time.

The trip back to the B&B was mostly silent, both talked out, both lost in thought. Dante's thoughts swirling around the fact that this birthday of hers had seemed to be some sort of full stop for her. While for him the Vine was clearly no longer an excuse to stay.

Time was truly ticking down now. He could feel it in his bones, in the thrum of his blood. The circumstances that had brought them together in this space, this time, would soon no longer be in play.

When he pulled up to the front of the Grape Escape, and Sutton didn't immediately get out of the car, instead leaning her head against the headrest and letting out a great sigh, Dante turned off the engine.

"I have something for you," he said.

Her smile was soft, her voice little above a whisper. "You do?"

"In case I saw you at some point today." He leaned into the back of the car, took the donut out of the container he'd put it into that morning. Then he stuck a single candle into the top.

She laughed, all delight, when he placed it on her upturned palm.

"Shh," he hushed her, pulling out a lighter. He cradled her hand in his, steadying her, and lit the wick.

Over the glow of the flickering flame, her soft

blue eyes were glossy, her smile radiant. "*Buon compleanno*, Sutton. Happy birthday."

"Dante, this is… I can't even…" But she could, and she did. Telling him how delighted, how touched, with every spark in her eyes, with the shape of her smile.

"Make a wish," he said.

She nodded, her face turning solemn as she closed her eyes, then blew out the flame in a short sharp puff. A sliver of smoke rose between them, a puff of white disappearing into the darkness.

The front porch light of the B&B was but a soft distant glow.

And Celia's words—*time to let go*—rang in his head. Not because they had been difficult to hear—although they were—but because they echoed what had become an insistent voice in the back of his head urging him to give himself grace for some time now.

Not to move on, but to move forward.

"To my mind," he said, his voice like gravel against the emotion pressing tight against his throat as his gaze roved over Sutton's lovely face, "that thing looks far too big for one person to eat."

Her gaze lifted to his, and she let out a huff of breath through her nose. As if she too was battling more emotion than she could contain.

Dante shifted, and leaned toward her, his hand sliding into the hair at the back of her head. "May I come up?"

"Dante," she said, eyes wide, lips parted, a thousand thoughts flittering across her face.

His thumb traced the curl of her ear. "May I come up?"

She nodded. Then said, "Yes. Please. Do."

He smiled, even while he felt like laughing. As if a simple yes from this woman was enough to unleash more joy than one simple man could possibly know what to do with.

Dante followed Sutton up the stairs of the sleeping inn.

He counted the places he wanted to kiss her— the jut of her shoulder bone, the dip of her neck. He watched the clip keeping her hair in a messy twirl atop her head, imagined removing it, feeling the cool silky weight of her hair in his hands.

When they reached the first landing, he took an extra step and rested a hand on her hip. She stopped as his thumb slid beneath the hem of her top. A heady sigh escaping her mouth.

He took it as a good sign and slid his hand around her front, grazing the dip of her navel, feeling her skin twitch beneath his touch.

"Hurry," she whispered, her hand over his as she guided him up the next lot of stairs.

Then a stair creaked, the light in the sconce flickering, and Sutton stopped, swearing lightly beneath her breath.

"Why are we tiptoeing?" Dante asked, loving

the way she shivered as his breath brushed over her neck.

"I'm worried about Barry."

He stopped her then, spinning her, two steps above him, to face him. "I'm sorry?"

"No!" she said, eyes bright as they roved over his eyes, his cheeks, before settling on his mouth. "Not in that way. If he knew you were here, he might insist on sitting you down and asking your intentions."

Dante moved up a step till they were flush against one another. His hand curving around her back, skin on skin.

"I'm happy to explain my intentions," he said, "to you."

"You have intentions?"

"I've had intentions for weeks now. Specific, well-thought-out, richly detailed intentions. I can share them with you now, in English and Italian, if that was your wish."

She held the donut in both hands, between them, like a chastity belt. "It wasn't my wish. Though it might be nice. Then again, I do like surprises."

His voice was a growl as he said, "Let's get a move on, then, shall we?"

With that he spun her, and hands spanning her hips, encouraged her up the stairs. She laughed as she found herself taking them two at a time. Then bit her lip, trying to keep her laughter in check, lest Barry show up and get in their way.

Naturally, her room was right at the top. A converted attic, no less. Once there, she passed him the donut, her fingers fumbling with the key. When she finally slid it into place, the opening of the door was like a flint to a stone.

Sutton's arms were around Dante's neck, donut and all, as he walked her backward, kissing her for all he was worth.

"Duck," she breathed, leaning back so he'd not hit his head. Then she tore his jacket from her shoulders, one arm at a time, and tossed it across the room while keeping the donut safe.

While Dante reached out with a foot and slammed the door closed. Barry be damned.

Then they had their arms around one another again, all hot breath and lush kisses. The room so small, the back of Sutton's knees hit the bed seconds later, and together they fell. Dante shifted at the last so as not to land on her, or the donut, and they hit the mattress in a twist of limbs, puffing breaths.

He lifted his hand, swept her hair from her eyes. To think, all those weeks of flirtation, finding excuses to spend time together, finding reasons why they should not, had led them to this moment.

"Tell me what you want, Sutton."

Her voice was a smidge above a whisper as she said, "I can't."

"Trust me, you can," he assured her, pressing a kiss to the tip of her nose.

"I don't mean I *can't* can't. I can't because it might ruin my birthday wish." She glanced quickly at the donut, as if hoping it wasn't listening.

If Dante's heart hadn't been hammering in his chest by then, it was now.

"And even though you're here," she went on, "considering we are us, I'm quietly terrified it still might not come true."

There was one sure way to prove to her she had nothing to worry about.

He shifted so he was up on one elbow, held out a hand. "Donut, *per favor.*"

She passed it to him, a miracle it had survived the trip. He reached out to place it carefully on the bedside table, where a lit lamp sent a soft arc of light over the bed, bar a shadow from whatever creature was leaning in its base.

"The bedside drawer," she said.

After a pause, Dante opened it to find empty lolly wrappers, brochures for Vermillion sights to see, and a box of condoms. Unopened.

He placed the box on the bed, and closed the drawer, then turned back to find she'd rolled onto her back, her hands over her head, her dark hair splayed out around her, having lost her hair clip along the way.

She glanced at the box, her tank top lifting at her waist as she moved, and staying there, revealing a sliver of pale skin above the low rise of her jeans. "Wishful thinking?"

"Not anymore," he assured her.

And when she smiled, his hammering heart swelled to fill his entire chest.

"Bellissima," he said as he looked at her. Then, *"Splendido, adorabile, dolce, spettacolare, affascinante."* And any number of endearments. None of which came close to touching on how seeing her there, wanting him, made him feel.

He ran a hand down the edge of her jaw, scooting past the edge of her lush mouth, which dropped open on a sigh. He traced the side of her neck, the ridge of her collarbone, the neckline of her top.

She writhed up into his touch, and his finger slipped beneath the fabric, tracing the swell of her breast. Then he hooked his fingers under the strap of her top and pulled it over her shoulder, revealing a soft pink bra strap. He leaned in, took it in his teeth and gave it a short twang, before he slipped it off her shoulder.

"Dante," she said, pulling his face into her neck. Her hands in his hair, tugging and holding him close as his tongue traced the swell of her breast, then the dark pink smudge at the edge of her nipple.

When he pushed the last of the fabric aside with his nose, she whimpered, and hooked her leg around his. Whispering his name, like an incantation. *"Dante, Dante, Dante..."*

With a growl that came from some deeply primal place inside him, he took her nipple in his mouth, sucking, licking, nipping. She cried out, and he took more, cupping her breast in his hand, the skin warm and velvet soft, as he opened his mouth to her, his tongue lapping at her in an age-old rhythm that had her arcing into him. Crying out. Telling him what she wanted in every way bar words.

Constricted, needing skin on skin, he moved onto his knees and whipped his shirt over his head. Her eyes were dark, unseeing, as she reached for him, running her hands down his chest, tracing the lower half of the vine tattoo that swept over his shoulder, scraping her nails over the ridges of his muscles, before curling her fingers into his jeans, yanking open the first two buttons and pulling him to her.

He fell forward, bracing himself once more. Then made it his mission to kiss every inch of her.

Her left breast, the skin now pink from the abrasion of his beard. The pair of moles beneath her right breast. The small appendix scar low on her belly. Rolling his tongue around her navel, catching on scars left by a once-upon-a-time belly ring, he hooked the button of her jeans through the buttonhole, and tugged at her fly.

Half-gone, lost to pleasure, even more of a sensualist than he'd imagined she would be, she lifted her hips helpfully as he tugged at her jeans, and slipped them over her feet.

Her underwear, white cotton, with a small bow at the top, was twisted from the fact she could not keep still. The apex damp. The scent of her desire, the way her legs rubbed against one another as if she was lost to pleasure already, had him cupping himself for a moment, breathing through a wave of need so strong he feared, for him, it might be over before it began.

"Dante," she said, as if it was the only word keeping her tethered.

"I'm here, *tesoro*," he whispered, running his hands down both legs, from hip to knee, pressing them apart. She lifted off the bed, her eyes smoky, then falling back spilled open for him.

Unable to wait another second to taste her, to own her, to make her birthday wish come true, he swept her underwear to one side, traced his finger down her centre, before following with a long, slow, flat sweep of his tongue. He took his time, dipping the tip of his tongue inside her, circling the bud above, and when she began to whimper, he took it between his lips and sucked. Lathed, and sucked. Lathed and sucked.

Till she bowed off the bed, her breath held, and he pressed her legs apart with his shoulders and took her centre in his mouth and held her there, tongue sweeping over her as she cried out. And cried out. And cried out.

When he felt her shuddering, he eased back. Only to realise she was laughing. Spent, her taut body flopping to the bed, her head fell back as she laughed and laughed and laughed.

He moved over her, to lay his length alongside hers, brushing aside the soft wisps of damp hair curling about her temples. Her eyes still dark with desire. Her face a picture of pure joy. And relief.

As her laughter eased, and their gazes caught, her body warm and syrupy soft, his suspended on the edge of need, it felt as if time stretched once again. As if the universe granted them extra, when they needed it most.

There was no rush. Certain when his time came it would be worth the wait.

A while later, after she'd told him stories of birthdays past, comparing them all with this one, Sutton sat on the edge of the bed with a sheet wrapped around her, donut in hand.

She tore it in half, as promised, and offered him the smallest portion.

"It's my birthday donut," she said with a shrug, before biting down on the thing, her eyes rolling back in her head in pleasure.

And Dante saw a future unspool before him. Rough-edged and out of focus, but filled with laughter, and time spent learning one another's desires, and pasts, and intimate moments such as this.

Tossing the donut over his shoulder, he grabbed

her, sheet and all, and pulled her onto his lap. His feet found the floor, at the end of the bed. She shifted till she straddled him, and wrapped the sheet around them both.

Then slid her hand between them, to unhook the last button of his jeans, slide her hand into his underwear, and free him with zero compunction.

Then, after swallowing the donut, and licking her fingers, she leaned in, wrapped her arms around his head, and kissed him hard, deep, wet. Rolling against him, till he could barely see straight.

When he felt himself teeter close to the edge, he lifted her to her knees, shucked off his jeans, and grabbed one of the rows of condoms from the box they'd moved to the middle of the bed.

There he made her wait, hovering so close, as he sheathed himself. When he nodded, she sank down over him, taking him in one go.

Her smile was impudent, confident. He rocked up into her, and her mouth opened on a gasp. Laughing, he slid a hand around her back, and rocked up into her again.

This time she was ready. And together they moved, slowly, incrementally, feeling every sensation, face-to-face. His hands sweeping her hair from her cheeks, holding her as he kissed her gently. Then more deeply. Her hands running through his hair, kneading his back, holding her to him when he changed the angle.

Till Dante felt Sutton clutch around him, her hands gripping his hair, her thighs quivering against his. Holding her through it, watching her face—eyes closed, skin pink—she teetered on the very edge of release, for an eternity, before collapsing against him with a whimper and a cry.

Holding her tight, he thrust once, twice. She shifted, one hand clutching his shoulder, the other braced against his knee, as she leaned back, taking him deeper than he'd imagined she could. Holding her there, taking her breast in his mouth, he came like a rocket. All power and heat, his vision nothing but stars.

Later, Sutton told him he was welcome to stay, then fell asleep the moment her head hit the pillow. Dante hadn't planned on going anywhere.

When he woke in the night, he found Sutton curled up into his chest.

He waited for the usual rolling litany of recriminations to pervade his mind—the long-held, deeply embedded voice telling him he did not deserve this much good. But wait as he might, none came.

Then, as if his stillness unsettled her, Sutton shifted. Her hand uncurling to lie gently over his heart. And from one beat of that heart to the next, he knew he'd never be the same again.

CHAPTER NINE

It was a good couple of hours before the Vine would open, yet she sat at the bar, drinking a milkshake and mooning over Dante while he made notes in the margin of an ancient occupational health and safety manual.

She knew it wasn't something he needed to do, just as she knew sitting around drinking milkshakes while mooning over the man wasn't sustainable as a lifestyle choice.

Sure, it had more than sustained the past week, to the point she'd had to make another trip to the chemist for a second box of condoms. But this man had not been on her "to-do list" when she'd bought the ticket and jumped on that plane. Or had he? Did it matter, when, in the long run, they both had real lives to get back to?

"This cannot be interesting," Dante said, in that gruff voice that she adored so very much. Especially when it was whispering sweet nothings in her ear as she fell apart in his arms.

Gaze tracing the column of his neck, she could

all but taste the salty tang, feel the delicious give of his skin when she scraped her teeth over the tendons. "You have no idea."

He looked up, his eyes dark, filled with smoke and memory, an aura of contentment for which she took complete ownership. *"Tesoro,"* he said, "I have every idea."

Kent, who had been walking behind Dante at the time, looked at Sutton with wide eyes, and mouthed, "Oh, my God!"

Sutton laughed into her milkshake and motioned for Dante to get back to work.

Then she tried her best to do the same; answering the slew of emails and messages she'd let slide the last few days. Something she never did. Even when touring, or unwell, she was a manic checker-inner with the bands she managed. The best, most connected, most present partner they could ever hope for.

Now she wondered if it had been less innate conscientiousness, and more due to the metaphorical hand of time that had been pressing her onward all these years. As such, for the past few days she'd put the living of her own life ahead of worrying about anyone else's first for a change. Living in the moment with Dante, knowing how special it was. That *he* was.

"You're watching me," Dante said, watching *her*. His chin in his hand, knuckles curled against his cheek. All dark eyes and ruggedly elegant beauty. "I can feel it."

"Lies. All lies," she said, picking up her phone, and finding a message she'd drafted to send to Bianca. "I am an independent woman, with hobbies and interests and obligations outside of this."

She flapped a hand at him, edited the message, and pressed Send.

Then, proving her words, she pulled up her socials, scrolled through posts about music festivals, images from live shows. She saved one post into her "photography" folder, thinking the imagery would really suit the Magnolia Blossoms.

The next post in line had a chill coming over her.

The headline read: "The Sweety Pies Cut Record New Record Deal under New Management."

Thing was, she'd been their manager for years.

Swiping to her contacts, she tried calling Landry, the lead singer. Nothing. She texted them a screenshot of the post, and a text shot straight back.

Ack. Sorry you had to see that.

So it's true?'

We wanted to tell you in person but you've been hard to get a hold of of late.

Ouch.

Sutton went to type something else, to explain, or to ask them to explain, considering she'd discovered them, nurtured them, guided them through so many near breakups. But her hands were shaking.

She closed her eyes for a moment, and centred her thoughts. She'd lost bands before, it was par for the course. So why did this change make her feel so adrift?

Because it was *them*? The shock of not being given the courtesy of a heads-up? Or because of who she had morphed into since coming to this place. The fierce, independent, go-getter now sensitive, unguarded, soft.

Another text hit her phone before she'd had the chance to come up with a response:

We're good, though, right? You always said you'd be fine if the time came we needed more.

Sutton let her phone drop slowly to the bar. She had said those words, more often than she could remember. In fact, she'd made a life out of walking away and not looking back. Thinking it made her tough, inured to personal pain. Never putting herself in a position to break, unlike like her dad. In love, or life.

But seeing it written that way—made her feel lonely, disappointed, and sad. And she didn't like it one single bit.

"Everything all right?" Dante asked, no doubt sensing her discomfort.

"Peachy," she said, blinking furiously to hold back the sting in the back of her eyes. "I'm just going outside to make a quick call."

She sent a quick screenshot to the Magnolia Blossom group chat, only for her phone to ring just as she hit the footpath.

"Wild, right?" Sutton asked, rubbing at her temples.

"Did you know?" Bianca asked. "I feel you'd have told us if you'd known."

Sutton shook her head, and all three Blossoms made it clear what they thought of how it had gone down.

Francie pushed Zhou and Bianca out of the frame. "Next time I see them, I'm going to... steal their mike stands."

Sutton laughed, then turned the phone away as she swiped at the stupid tear that had spilled from nowhere.

"You okay?" Bianca asked.

"Yeah. Of course. Just in shock, I guess. But it's fine. It will be fine. I mean, you guys know that I support whatever decisions you believe you have to make for yourselves. I've always been upfront about that. I just hope, if you ever feel it's time, that you'd say so—"

"Never!" said Bianca, holding the phone close to her face. "You are our ride or die. We'd not be here without you and we love you. And that's the end of that."

"Okay," said Sutton, the emotions rushing through her strange, and disconcerting in their enormousness. As if the past few days spent with Dante had turned on some tap she didn't know how to turn off. "If you're about to suggest we get matching tattoos, I get final say on the design."

"Boo," said Bianca. Then, "Oh, and while I have you, your dad messaged me. He asked if I knew of any walking tours in my neck of the woods."

Sutton blinked. "In *the Netherlands*?"

"Yep! He said he and a friend were out to lunch, talking about walking holidays, and were 'collating a list of possible future adventures.' How cool is that?"

Out to lunch, with a friend. This from a man who'd not dated, as far as Sutton knew, since the day she was born. How much more of her world would be upside down when she got back? If she waited much longer, it might not be recognisable at all.

"So cool," Sutton managed. "Now don't forget to send through any photos, video, et cetera of the Liefdescafé shows, okay? Hope they go brilliantly!"

Zhou said. "Will do!"

"We miss you!" Bianca added.

"Next time we expect real tea!" Francie insisted. "The dirty stuff!"

With that they rang off, and Sutton gripped her phone for a few long seconds as the news upon news upon news swirled and settled inside her.

When she glanced up through the windows of the Vine and Stein, she could just make out Dante talking on the phone. His expression was cool, his movements spare and strong, his brow furrowed in that gorgeously Dante way as he listened without interrupting.

And just like that all feelings of sadness, and loneliness, dissolved away.

While that should have felt like a good thing, the best thing, she felt herself begin to tremble. All over. Knowing that when the time came to walk away from that man, *not* looking back would be an impossibility.

Dante hung up the call from his aunt. His blood felt cool, thick, as he held his phone for a long moment, then ran a hand over his mouth as he looked up to see Sutton was once again pacing, as she took another call, through the glass.

The way she curled her hair around a finger, kicked at the ground, looked up, and smiled as a stranger passed her by—he knew he'd never be able to see such movement from another person and not think of her.

How soon that time came did not feel up to him. Not anymore. For the moment he'd gotten over himself enough to let her into his heart, he was done. And he knew, in that same heart, that she felt the same way.

The problem was, there were more than two of them in this relationship, and always had been. His aunt and cousins, her father, the Vine staff, their new friends in Vermillion, his people back at Sorello, the bands who relied on her—they all tugged, and begged for attention, and got in the way.

And now…

He looked once more at his phone, as he heard the snick of the front door.

"Hey!" she said, her hair lifting and falling as she strode his way and pulled herself back onto her stool. Then, "You okay? You look as if you've seen a ghost."

"It is. I think. I…" He put his phone into his pocket and rounded the bar. Pulling up the stool beside hers. "My aunt just called. Apparently, she has been mulling over your conversation, from the night you came for dinner. Specifically, your mother's name."

Sutton stilled, the blood rushing from her face. "Oh?"

Dante reached out and took her hand, gently rubbing warmth into her fingers as they lay limply in his hold. "Apparently her name rang a bell, the other night. Turns out there is a Mya Hawthorn—an artist, a potter—who lives in the next town."

Sutton shook her head. "Did you say 'lives'? As in…present tense?"

Dante nodded.

"Wow," said Sutton, eyes wide. "I mean, it could be a relative, right?"

Dante breathed out. "Celia has met her. At a fundraiser a few years ago. She said she would be the right age…to be your mother."

Sutton pulled her hand back, curling it against her chest. Swallowing hard, she shook her head. "That might be, but… I mean, she wasn't intimating that this Mya could be my actual mother?" She shook her head, hard. "My mother died. When she was twenty-eight. Sending my father in a spiral of romantic despair, that he apparently is only just now coming out of."

Her gaze slid over his shoulder, far away, as she whispered, "Now that he knows that I am here."

"Sutton—"

Shaking her head, she slid from the chair, looked around, grabbed her backpack from under her stool, and slung it over her shoulder.

"Sutton—" He tried again.

She held up a hand; gaze hard, shining like glass holding back a wash of tears. "Your aunt is wrong. Or lying. Or… I don't know." Her hand balled in a fist at her belly. "Oh. This just feels too cruel."

Dante's hands clenched and unclenched at his sides, uncertain how to help her. "My aunt is a lot of things," he said, "but she is not cruel."

Sutton shook her head, then turned and strode toward the front door.

"Where are you going?" Dante called. "Let me drive you. Or I can find this woman. Talk to her for you—"

Sutton stopped at the door. "Don't, please. Just give me some space, to figure this out."

"So long as you know you don't have to do it alone." Dante waited for her to turn, to change her mind. To need him, as he'd come to need her.

Only she swept out the door and didn't look back.

An hour later, Sutton stood outside Artisan Row, a creative collective in Griffin, about ten minutes down the road from Vermillion.

The hand gripping the strap of her backpack felt about as damp as her mouth felt dry, and her insides twisted over on themselves as she turned that last conversation with Dante over and over in her head.

Should she have let him come with her? Had she been too dismissive? The thing was, he wasn't her partner, or even her boyfriend. He was a crush she was sleeping with a thousand miles from home.

Okay, so Dante was more than that. Much more. But that was the problem! He was some magical, unicorn, fairy-tale, grumpy, gorgeous winemaker from some halcyon pocket of delight in the heart of Italy, for Pete's sake!

While this—this *mess*, this possibility, this thread of discomfort in her belly—was her real life. And she'd come to Vermillion looking for connection to her past, not some mythical magical future.

Careful what you ask for, she thought as she sucked in a deep breath and forced herself to walk through a twisty series of stone paths, and cute hedgerows, and garden statues, and caravans filled with handmade art.

Bracing herself against whatever was to come, calling on whatever inner steel she had at her disposal, she turned a corner to find a garden filled with hundreds of pots. All kinds of pots. And a hand-burned wooden sign reading Pots by Mya Hawthorn.

Her stomach tumbled, knotting in on itself as dread and hope intermingled inside her. She took every effort to haul herself in.

Was it possible, actually possible, that she was about to meet her mother? *Her mother!* Alive. If so, her life's philosophy, all those years spent racing against time, were based on a myth. Which, ironically, the past week she'd let go—being still, living in the moment, finding contentment in doing not much at all. And it had been wonderful.

Then, *Bam!* Fate stepped in and smacked her across the back of the head.

Stairs led to a small cottage with a front porch covered in ivy, and laden with pots hanging in crocheted baskets. Only way to know for sure was to go inside, only her feet wouldn't move.

Couldn't.

Until Dante's words came back to her, his voice strong with understanding, as if he was used to taking the big emotional hits so that others didn't have to. *"So long as you know you don't have to do it alone."*

It was enough for her to take the first step.

A bell tinkled as she walked through the door. The space was overflowing with baskets filled with wool, shelves stacked with crockery, vases, plant pots of all shapes and sizes. She could barely get her bearings before a woman walked through a door behind the small counter, wringing a towel around her hands.

She wore a yellow, paint-splattered apron over a knotty knitted jumper, denim overalls, and khaki gumboots. She'd used a paintbrush to twirl her long wavy hair—once dark, now salt-and-pepper—into a loose bun.

Sutton's father had no photos of her mother, his memory of her "strong enough." His descriptions, when Sutton had pressed, ran to "dramatic, ethereal and gifted." Nothing ethereal about this woman—she was real. Right there. Flesh and blood.

And when she looked up, and spotted Sutton, it was like looking into her own eyes.

"Hey, honeybun," the woman said, her face creasing as she smiled. "What you looking for?"

Sutton nearly choked, hearing her father's endearment in this stranger's voice. She opened her mouth, but nothing came out. Some huge writhing thing inside her stopping her from speaking. Waiting for this woman Mya Hawthorn to put two and two together on her own.

See me. Recognise me. Make me believe that you are why I came here. Give me the connection, the foundation, the feeling that I'm home I've probably been searching for my whole life.

But the woman only cocked her head, and waited.

Sutton licked her lips, lifted her chin, and said, "I'm… Are you Mya Hawthorn?"

"That's me," the woman said, giving an empty shelf beside her a quick wipe so she could then fill it with knitted knickknacks.

"My name is Sutton. Sutton Mayberry. I think… I think perhaps you once knew my father."

The woman's hands stopped fussing. Her eyes widening imperceptibly, before she turned and looked deep into Sutton's eyes. Then cool as you please, she said, "How is Gerard these days?"

"He's well," Sutton found herself saying, even

as tears welled inside her, as if filling her from her toes all the way to her chest.

And where she wanted to say to this woman, *Did he leave you? Did you leave him? Does he even know you're alive? He's lonely. He misses you. He mourns you. I mourn you,* Sutton thought, voicing something that had never explicitly occurred to her. But it was true. Not having known her mother, she'd spent a lifetime chasing her down.

Instead, she found herself saying, "He's planning a walking tour, through the Netherlands, with his friend. Marjorie."

"That sounds like something he'd enjoy," said Mya, not unkindly. "And you? What brings you here?"

"I'm sorry," said Sutton, closing her eyes, holding out her hand as she attempted to get her bearings. "I'm sure you can imagine this is all rather a lot for me to take in. I... I was led to believe that you were dead."

Mya let out a long breath. Then, moving a roll of brown butcher paper from a chair, motioned for Sutton to sit down. Sutton did, her legs giving way as soon as they had permission to do so.

"I'm going to make us a cuppa. Vanilla? Caffeine-free suit?"

About as much as a glass of wine, Sutton thought, holding back a slightly hysterical laugh. "Sounds fine."

Tea served, Mya sat on the chair opposite Sutton's, curling a foot up beneath her. While Sutton absorbed everything about her that she could— looking for signs, for similarities, while waiting for a torrent of anger, of futility, of sorrow to whip up inside her.

But she felt nothing. Perhaps she was numb, in some deep self-protect mode. Or it was all backing up inside her, waiting for the right moment to break loose.

"Sutton. I always thought that was such a pretty name. Your father chose it, you know? What did you come here looking for today?"

"I'm not sure. Maybe the truth."

Mya looked at her then, for quite a long beat. Gaze raking over her hair, her face, her clothes. Was *she* searching for similarities? Imagining herself the same age? The age at which this woman had died in Sutton's mind.

Because her father…

No, she couldn't go there. Couldn't think about his complicity in the falsehood. Not now. Not yet.

"Truth is a slippery thing," said Mya with a soft smile. "Altered by time, memory, repetition, the needs of the players involved. All I can safely say is that your father wanted more from me than I had to give."

Sutton flinched. Not because Mya's words were harsh, for they were gently offered. They were so close to the words Dante had said to her the night she'd first kissed him. The night he'd tried to stop things going further. As if he knew the day was already nearing when it had to end.

"So you *left* him?" Sutton asked.

And me, she thought. *You also left me.* Which was an awful thing. Wasn't it? This woman certainly didn't seem torn up about it.

"No," Mya said, her voice gentle yet assured, "I suggested it would be better for him, and for you, if he left. This was my home. *Is* my home. I needed for it to remain that way."

Sutton shook her head, slowly, back and forth. Trying to make sense of this woman's absolute certainty that she'd made the right choice. Her peace of mind—even in the face of seeing the daughter she'd abandoned.

Maybe that would take another twenty-eight years to understand.

Sutton felt a kind of numbness come over her at the thought. Really? Was she willing to do that all over again? Chase understanding of someone else's choices rather than make her own?

Again, she found her mind tipping to Dante. To the choices ahead of them both. Her tongue felt thick in her mouth, as she asked, "What did that mean—that my father wanted more than you had to give?"

Mya leaned forward. "I never wanted to be a wife, or a mother, I just wanted to live a life that filled me with a sense of purpose. While your father wanted security, assurances, promises I had no hope of keeping. Does that make any sense?"

More than Sutton cared to admit.

Mya and her father were complete opposites. Had different energies, different visions, different post codes, different goals. Neither love, nor a child, had been enough to combat that.

"Do you have any regrets?" Sutton asked, knowing it was the one truth that she needed to know.

Mya reached out, and wrapped a cool hand around Sutton's wrist. "I regret none of it," said Mya. "Not the relationship, not you, nor the fact that we went our separate ways. Not for a moment."

Sutton nodded, believing her, and sipped her tea.

Dante paced the office of the Vine, wearing a path into the floor.

It had been hours since Sutton had left. He could wait outside the B&B, or drive the streets until he found her, only he had no idea if she'd gone looking for Mya Hawthorn, gone for a drive to clear her head, or if she'd *gone*…period.

And it was his fault.

Not directly, he knew that. But partly, certainly. He could have shared Celia's news in a different way, a different place. Instead, he'd charged in like a wounded bear, without nuance or sensitivity, only certain it was too important to keep it from her.

Now she was out there somewhere, hurting, confused, alone.

Not that he thought she'd do anything foolish. Or put herself in harm's way. But then he'd never imagined Isabella going that far either.

Dante rubbed both hands over his face and growled, hating this feeling of utter helplessness.

It was not the same. He *knew* it was *not the same*. Try telling his heart that—caught as it was in a loop of flight or fright, spinning him back in time to how it felt as his feet sank into the mud, sucking at him, making it near impossible to get to her. To *Isabella*. Face down in the dam.

Sutton was a grown woman; strong, resilient. She faced down dragons every day of her career, and woke the next ready to face more. He'd never known anyone who could ride the waves of life's ups and downs with more grace, humour, and delight than she.

Yet when his phone rang, and he saw Sutton's number on the screen, his relief was so strong he moaned. "Sutton."

"Hey." Her voice was soft. Tired.

"Where are you?"

"In the car. Pulled over halfway between Griffin and home."

Home. Dante knew she had a complicated relationship with that word. The fact that she'd used it now cut deep. Home for her was not about place, but people. Home, in that moment, meant him.

"Can I come get you?" he asked, hand tugging at his hair.

"I'm okay. I just needed to hear a friendly voice."

Feeling anything but friendly, Dante pressed his hand over his mouth.

"I found her," she said, into the silence. "Mya Hawthorn. My mother."

Dante twisted and sat on the arm of the couch. *Hell. Just...hell.* "Have you spoken to your father?"

"It's four in the morning over there."

"Still, I'm sure he'd understand."

"I'll wait till morning."

Morning meant several hours of being alone with this news. Of feeling in limbo. A terribly lonely place to be. And even while he knew he should be facilitating her needs, he needed to see her. To be sure she was all right. To know she was safe.

"Can I see you tonight?" he asked. "To listen, or hold you, or just be there."

The phone stayed silent for several long beats before he heard her sob. "Actually, can you come? Can you come get me?"

Dante had his car keys in hand before she finished the request.

CHAPTER TEN

EYES CLOSED, Sutton heard the crunch of tyres on gravel, then the slam of Dante's car door.

When without preamble he opened her door, and held out a hand, she took it, stepping into his big, strong arms. She pressed her face to his chest, drinking in the dry, earthy scent of him. Hands catching on the warm, familiar weave of his flannelette shirt. And as his coarse palms caught on her hair as he stroked her, and he murmured comforting words in a language she barely understood, she felt so much. Too much. Especially when compared with all the *nothing* she'd been feeling the past few hours.

It was enough for her to pull back.

Placing her hands flat against his chest, she gently pushed him away. Giving herself space to breathe. To think. To consider for once, rather than going with the flow.

"Thank you for coming," she said, then, "I'm not even sure why I called—"

"I'm glad you did."

She ran a hand through her hair and took another step back. It was a moment before he slid his hands into the pockets of his jeans, when he clearly wanted to be holding her still.

"I think I'm okay to drive now. If you follow?"

"Are you sure? I can organise for someone else to pick up your car."

She breathed out, the tumult inside her slowly settling. "I'm sure."

"And where do you wish to go?"

"Back to the B&B, I think. I should eat. Hunker in for a bit to get my head around all of this." Then, after a beat, she added, "Would you… Could you come with me?"

His eyes, those deep dark chocolate penetrating depths, filled with such raw emotion she felt the hit of it right in the centre of her chest. An explosion of warmth, of feeling, of happiness and heart pain. As if he alone knew how to unlock the more vulnerable places inside her, the ones she'd been all too happy to keep hidden, keep safe.

If she'd taken one thing from finding her mother, from Mya Hawthorn's calm certainty that things were exactly as they ought to be, was that giving someone the key to loving you meant they had the key to hurt you.

Still, when Dante caught her eye, and smiled at her, waiting patiently for what she needed, she said, "Come. And stay."

Dante reached for her, hauled her close once more, kissed her atop her head, then helped her back into the car.

Later that night, Sutton lay curled up in Dante's arms, her leg resting over his, his meaty bicep a pillow beneath her head.

While Dante had been breathing softly, rhythmically, for some time, she was a million miles from sleep. Her brain was all knots, and electric sparks, and rabbit holes, determined to fix every problem on her plate before it could shut down.

The Magnolia Blossoms were off having fun without her, while the Sweety Pies had left her. Her dad was making big plans in his life, for the first time ever, and she wasn't there to help. Her dad, the one person she trusted above all others, had been lying to her for all these years. Her mother was alive, and unrepentant.

It was a lot. And Sutton had spent her adult life avoiding "a lot." Taking on just enough work to enjoy it without ever really stretching herself. Keeping lovers at arm's length—friendly, never serious, as off she went to the next city, the next adventure, with a smile and a wave. Telling herself it was so she had time to experience as many facets of life as she could in her time on earth.

Dante shifted, a growl rising from his chest even in sleep.

Could she really do the same to him? Smile, and wave, and leave.

She tipped her head the smallest amount to press a gentle kiss to his warm, bronzed skin, and could feel the Italian sunshine that had made him that way. Smell the soil, the leaves, the tannin of the grapes that had given him calluses on his hands, and built up the muscles on his bones.

She slowly moved the sheet, tracing the edge of his beautiful tattoo, tenderly, so as not to wake him. She flattened her hands over the slabs of his large pecs. Fingers catching in the light smattering dark curling hair that arrowed over his rib cage. Lower.

When his skin retracted from her touch, a slight hiss dragging between his teeth, she lifted her head, but his eyes remained closed.

She laid her hand on his chest, and rested her chin on her hand, and looked at him. The dark lashes creating a smudge against his cheeks. The dark stubble, throwing auburn and flecks of silver in the low glow of the Minotaur lamp.

She could think in circles all she wanted, but the truth was she had to go back to her real life soon. As did he. And they'd both be okay. Surely. Like any holiday romance, it couldn't possibly feel as big, as acute, as important later on as it did while in the midst of it.

"What is going on in that head of yours?" Dante

asked, lifting his head and placing his spare arm beneath. "I can *feel* you thinking dire thoughts."

"I'm thinking about my mother," Sutton said. Which was, at least, partly true.

"What about her?"

"She was so unruffled by my appearance. So settled in her decision to let us go. I should be a mess, right now, right?" *Angry, desolate, hurt— something.* "Instead, I feel as if she could have been a woman who ran a pot shop, and nothing more." Her eyes swung back to his. "Is that healthy? Or a sign that I'm missing some basic human ingredient?"

Dante rolled so that they faced one another, nose to nose, limbs wrapped loosely over one another. The hand on her chest, dropped and curled backward, against his heart.

"Self-protection is a pretty powerful human ingredient. Yes, it can keep people from getting too close, but it also stops them from having the capacity to hurt us. Something we are both rather adept at, I believe. Or at least I was. And then I met you."

Sutton swallowed, her throat tightening, the backs of her eyes hot and scratchy.

Smiling and frowning, all at once, Dante lifted a hand to brush her hair from her face. His fingers traced down her cheek, his thumb tugging at her lower lip before he leaned in and kissed her. Softly. As if marking his place. Marking her.

"You know the Vine does not need my help anymore, yet I am still here. Just as I know there will be no *second* dates for you, yet you are still here."

Knowing where he was going, and unable to control the rush of feeling rising inside her—so much everything compared with all the nothing—she shook her head, just the once. One final flash of self-protection before it burned to ash.

"You care for me, Sutton."

"I don't." Then, "I mean, I *do*. Of course I do. Just not... Not in the way I think you are intimating. I mean, I can't... I don't think I'm able." Her voice broke at the last. How was that for a truth that had been living inside her for as long as she could remember?

Dante's smile only grew.

"You care for me," he said, again, his fingers now sliding into her hair, sending ribbons of pleasure from her scalp to her centre. "You care for me, and I care for you. We both fought it, to no avail."

He moved so that her leg was tucked around his hip. Moved so that her chest was flush against his. Moved so that pleasure shot up in a thousand places on her body in such a visceral rush she began to tremble.

"Soon I'll be heading back to my vineyard, on a hill, near a small town, in the heart of my country, and you'll be back whizzing all over the world with your music, but that does not mean—"

"Stop," she said, lifting a hand to his mouth when the burning in the back of her eyes threatened to give way to actual tears.

He took her literally. His hand softening in her hair, the slow undulation of his hips ceasing on a breath. And the world seemed to teeter in that moment.

On one side, she could rest her head against this chest and tell him all her wild and frantic fears, and he would listen, and everything from that moment would be new and unknown and out of her control.

On the other side, it was time to say goodbye to the beautiful oblivion that was Vermillion, and step back into the life she'd known till now.

She moved her hand from his lips, and held his cheek. "Stop talking," she said, "and kiss me."

A beat slunk by, a beat in which she knew he knew the tumult inside her. Then he rolled over her, bracing himself so as not to crush her.

Brushing her hair off her face, he looked deep into her eyes. Then he kissed her; gently, on the tip of her nose, the curve of her cheek, on one closed eyelid, then the other. Then, while she hovered on the verge of sweet luxuriation, he kissed her. His tongue tracing the seam of her lips, before sweeping deep into her mouth.

Her arms slid around his neck as she pulled him close. Curling into his big, hard body, needing as much of him as she could get. For he knew what he was doing, conjuring delicious warmth in her limbs, waves of pleasure that lapped at her doubts, wearing them down.

Only he had no idea how deep her self-protection went.

Even as they moved and sighed in one another's arms, as her feeling for him swelled and grew, her mind wheeling with adoration and desire, falling into the picture he'd been offering her, all she could think was:

So much. Too much.

Even as all thought and feeling coalesced into a declivous ball of heat and joy and maybe even love, spilling out to her extremities and back again in waves of the purest of pleasure, some small part of herself baulked. Held back. Hunkered down. Tried with all its might to hold tight.

As Dante slept, a deep, unfettered sleep, Sutton lay staring at the ceiling and let the tears fall. The streams pooled in her ears before spilling to the damp pillow at her back. For finally the disparate threads in her mind had twirled into one perfect string.

She'd thought the inconsistency of the music industry suited her so well because she was able to cope with change.

She'd thought the fact she'd come out of meeting her mother feeling so little pain was down to that willful self-control.

She'd thought her romantic relationships never

amounted to anything serious because she had *decided* she would never put herself in a position to end up like her beloved dad. Broken by love, lost to the past.

She'd thought it had all been by choice.

What if it wasn't? What if it was innate? What if she held back, because she did not have it in her to let go? To be open to more. To love deeply. Truly. In a forever kind of way.

Something cracked inside her as it all came together in a bright burning truth. And where moments earlier she'd felt such comfort, such safety, such warmth in the arms of the beautiful man sleeping beside her, cold rushed in.

Maybe her choices had *never* been about avoiding her father's experiences. Maybe she'd been her mother's daughter all along.

Dante woke to find Sutton packing her bags.

His first thought was that maybe she was simply tidying up. She was a "clothes piled up on the chair in the corner are clean" kind of person. Not that he minded—he was a buy-five-of-the-same-shirt-and-two-of-the-same-jeans kind of guy.

Till he stretched, made a sound to go with it, and saw her gaze when it snapped his way. Shrouded. Dusty. As if her mind was only half in the room.

It had been a big twenty-four hours. Meeting her mother, processing the seed he'd hoped he'd planted in her mind—finding a way for this not to end when they went back to their real lives. Finding a way to make it last. Forever if she'd have him.

"Tesoro," he said, his morning voice gruff, as he leaned up on an elbow and ran a hand through his hair.

She narrowed her eyes at him, her lips thin.

"What?" he asked, laughter in his voice. In his soul. Something he'd never have expected, or asked for. Now he knew he did not want to live without it.

Her hand flapped at him, violently. "Why do you have to look like that?"

"Like what?" he asked, glancing down at his bare torso. He scratched at the edge of his tattoo.

She made a sound halfway between a groan and a growl. "All warm, and big, and hot…and you."

"I apologise," he said. "I will do my best not to be any of those things in future."

On the word *future*, she flinched. Which was his first sign that something might be seriously amiss. He lifted the sheet, his legs swinging to the floor, when she held up a hand.

"Stay. Please. I can't do this otherwise."

He let the sheet drop over his lap, and curled his fingers around the edge of the mattress. "Sutton," he said, "would you like to tell me what is going on?"

"I'm leaving."

He looked once more to her now frantic packing, and felt a tug of something slippery inside him. Like he was reaching for a ribbon, only for it to keep fluttering out of his grip. "By leaving you mean…"

"*Leaving* leaving. Going back to the UK. I should see my dad, to talk to him in person."

"You could call him—"

She shook her head. "No. It has to be in person. Then I have to go to the Netherlands to meet up with the Magnolia Blossoms, make sure they're being treated right by the manager of the place they're playing. I should rightly have been there all along anyway. Then I should go to Dublin to see the Sweety Pies. Beg them to take me back. Either way, it's past time I got back to real life. You should too."

"You're right," he said. "In fact, I was hoping we might be able to leave together. That you might wish to return by way of Umbria. So that I can show you Sorello. It's then only a two-and-a-half-hour flight from Perugia to London."

Dragging at a zip that was clearly caught on something, she barely seemed to hear him, so he added, "I looked it up. Some time ago, actually."

Her eyes drifted closed, and her fingers gripped the edge of her bag. "Dante," she said, "can we just not? Can we just agree that this was fun? A lovely, unexpected side benefit for the both of us.

A holiday fling, if you will. We can then go our separate ways grateful to have met."

Grateful to have *met*?

Dante reached out, grabbed his jeans from the floor by the bed. Forgoing underwear, he slid them on and went to her. Taking her by the elbows, and turning her to face him. "Can you slow, for just a moment? Tell me what has happened to send you into such a spin."

"This is not a spin," she said. "This is me finally snapping out of whatever whim brought me here. Leaving my life back home to fall apart without me."

She lifted her elbows from his grip and he let her. Then he placed a finger under her chin and tipped her face back to meet his. Her eyes blazed as she looked up at him, but he could feel her trembling all over.

While all kinds of words, and questions, and negations spilled onto the back of his tongue, he knew that she wasn't in any state to hear them. So, he took her hand and led her to the bed, where she slumped at the end, shoulders hunched, hands in her face.

Dante crouched down before her. His hand on her knee to keep her tethered. Connected to him. As he felt, deep in his bones, that if he did not, she would fly away, and he would lose her forever.

"Can we slow down for a moment?"

"Slow down? Dante, in my entire life, I've never

been as slow as I have been the past few weeks. And maybe that's the problem," she said, her hand flinging out dramatically, her knees now juddering as if she had a surfeit of energy she couldn't contain. "Way too much thinking time."

He lifted a hand, pressed his thumb to the middle of her forehead, and gave it a gentle push. She rocked back an inch, and stopped jiggling.

"What was that for?"

"My attempt to help you focus on one thing at a time." *Me*, he thought, holding her gaze. *Focus on me*. "Whatever has you spooked, *tesoro*, it will pass. All burdens do, eventually." Leaving space in the cracks for hope and happiness to flourish and grow.

Only Sutton seemed to be fracturing before his eyes. All cracks, no sunshine.

"Talk to me," he said. "Tell me what's wrong."

"What's *wrong*? Me! Clearly I am. Look at you."

She held out her hands, as if about to cradle his face, only to curl her fingers into her palms and shake them at the sky. As if touching him would undo her completely.

"You are so wonderful, Dante, and generous. Look at what you have done for your aunt. For the staff at the Vine. Because you are an exceptional human. So diligent, and…and responsible. You are a homeowner! While I'm so terrified of wanting stability, I sleep on strangers' couches more often than any twenty-seven...no twenty-eight-year-old should."

Dante would not have imagined being called a homeowner could feel like an insult, yet he was well aware she had flung it at him like a grenade. Even as he felt parts of himself begin closing up, like shutters against a storm, he dredged up a smile. "I think you'll find that Sorello is more of an estate, than a mere home. If that helps."

Sutton, who had been lost inside what maelstrom was inside her head, blinked. Then coughed out a laugh. Then a tear slid from her right eye.

Dante winced at the sight. Emotion now battering him from all sides. Emotion he was not equipped to handle. To abate. To fix. So much pressure, being the one upon whom another person's spirit depended. What if he was getting it wrong? The outcome could be catastrophic.

He felt himself sway away. And saw the moment she noticed.

She blinked against the glistening in her eyes, and took in a deep breath. When he opened his mouth to speak, she curled herself away from the bed, managing not to touch him as she moved back to her bags and kept on packing.

And for the first time in an awfully long time, Dante knew what true fear felt like.

Dante stood from his crouch, his knees groaning, bones protesting. Even his blood felt pained, as if tainted with acid. While his mind felt as scattered as his clothes, strewn about the room. Needing to feel something concrete, something real he could count on, he gathered them, put them on.

Then stood, tugging at his hair. "So, this is it?" he asked.

"I think it has to be. For both our sakes."

He breathed out hard, nodded, then made his way to Sutton's bedroom door.

"Dante?"

He stopped, and turned to find her watching him, her eyes wide, mouth downturned. "You'll thank me for this," she said. "I'm sure of it. I've spent my life avoiding tangles, while you've held on to your thorns like lifelines. Neither of us came here in any way prepared for this. For us."

Then, lovely face solemn, Sutton walked to him, placed a soft hand over his heart, lifted onto her tiptoes, and pressed a kiss to his cheek. "Thank you."

"For what?" he asked, feeling like his vision was filled with dust.

"For holding my hand through this most ill-thought-out of pilgrimages. I'm certain it wouldn't have been half as fun, half as satisfying, half as meaningful without you in it."

He offered a nod, then let himself out of her room, and out of her life.

Only half-aware of his surroundings as he jogged down the stairs of the B&B—trying not to remember kissing her on one landing, carrying her over another—then out the front door, and into the early morning light, his thoughts stray shrapnel in his head.

Once upon a time he'd retreated to a hillside lair, hiding away from all who knew him best, all who might look to him with regret or blame in their eyes. He'd cut himself off from family, from kinship, from partnership. As punishment.

Now, as he walked away from Sutton Mayberry, and all the delight, and humour, and warmth, and companionship that being with her had promised, he knew that solitude had been the easy way out.

CHAPTER ELEVEN

As soon as Dante shut her bedroom door, Sutton hunched over her bag. Her hands cramped, her entire body shook, as she did her all not to cry. Or hyperventilate.

She'd done the right thing, not letting it get any more serious than it already had. If she'd been a *better* person she'd not have let it get this far.

She'd spent so long finding ways not to get hurt, it had never occurred to her she had the ability to hurt someone else. Now all she could hope was that his feelings weren't as far down the track as hers had gone. Which, now he was gone, she could admit to herself was all the way.

Her phone pinged. Then pinged again.

While Dante had slept, spread out over her big soft bed, looking like some heavenly giant, she'd messaged everyone to let them know she was coming back. As if she knew she wouldn't be strong enough to do so without backup.

She picked up her phone, and with thumbnail lodged between her teeth, she started with Laila.

You can't leave, friend!

Then...

At least not without one final blowout at the Vine. Some grand, banger of a night filled with cocktails, and, naturally, some kind of means to collect email addresses for my mailing list.

Next message was from her dad.

She'd told Dante she wanted to see him in person, but the honest truth was she was terrified. Terrified she'd never forgive him. Terrified he'd solidify the fear she was just like her mother.

Only now, having sent Dante away, she felt flayed. As if she'd torn Band-Aids off every inch of skin. Calling her dad couldn't possibly make her feel worse.

She pressed the call icon, sat on the corner of the bed, and waited.

"Honeybun," said her dad, with his lovely accent, and smiley kindness. "It's been too long."

"Dad," she said, clutching her arm to her belly.

And while she'd spent the past twenty-four hours in such turmoil, hearing his voice she only felt love, and certainty that whatever his explanation was it would all be okay. For while her mother had sent them away, this man had cared for her with all his might.

"Are you at home?"

"Of course, love."

"Are you sitting down?"

Her father's silence was telling. As if he knew what was coming.

"I met someone yesterday," she said. "I met Mya Hawthorn."

She heard her father sigh. "Oh, love. I hoped… Well, I'm sure you know what I hoped. I can't even begin to apologise for how confronting that must have been. Oh, the thoughts you must have had about me. How upset with me you must be."

"No!" Then, swiping a finger under her eyes. "I mean, I was surprised. And hurt. And confused? Can you explain your side—why you chose not to tell me the truth?"

"You've met her," he clarified, his voice deadpan.

And, unexpectedly, Sutton felt laughter bubble in her belly. "She was rather open about her lack of interest, in either of us."

"Hmm. Something that became obvious over the months we were together. I tried to change her mind. For your sake, as much as mine. I did love her. Do still, I fear."

"I know."

"I never wanted you to think that you were not the most loved and lovable child that has ever been."

Sutton breathed out hard. "You certainly did that." Then, "Am I like her, do you think?"

"Are you *like* her? In what way?"

"I've never settled. With anyone. I expect people to move on, and I do the same, super-fast,
when they do. Do you think I even have it in
me…to love?"

"My girl! You are love. You are fiercely protective, loyal, selfless, devoted. You have dedicated
your life to standing up for those under your care.
To your own detriment at times. I feel as if this is
the right moment to point that out. Your mother
kept her life to herself, and herself alone. You're
as similar to *her* as I am to a pot plant."

Sutton laughed, as she was meant to do. And in
someplace deep down inside, she felt a flicker of
a flame come back to life. A kind of screw you,
to anyone telling her she was insufficient in some
way. Including herself.

"Is it wrong to say here that I think you are
rather like me? You don't suffer fools, won't waste
your precious time on anything you don't see as
worthy of it. One day you'll meet someone, the
right someone, someone strong, and joyous, who
adores you and keeps you close. Someone who
makes your heart grow three sizes bigger. Then
you'll know how different you and your mother
truly are."

Sutton wiped her nose, and blinked to clear the
tears from her eyes.

How could she tell him she'd already met someone just like that? That she'd walked into a bar in

Vermillion, spied a gorgeous, dark-haired Roman god of a man, a big hot bear with a thorn in his paw who looked at her as if she was the sunshine in his life, and turned her blood to fizz. And despite all that she'd already pushed him out the door?

Sutton ran a hand over her face, and gave her head a big shake. "On that," she said, "how is Marjorie?"

Her father's laugh was gentle, and warm. "When you told me where you were, it was a wake-up call. How small I have made my life, out of fear of having my heart broken again. And so, in an effort at being brave, like my daughter, I have booked that walking tour you told me about it."

"Oh, Dad. That's wonderful."

"So, if you were thinking of coming to visit over the next couple of weeks, I'm sorry, but I won't be here."

She laughed louder now. "Fair enough."

"Are we okay, you and me?" her dad asked, his voice unsteady, as if he knew things had changed a little between them, as they had changed in himself.

"Always."

After promising to call again the next day, with concrete plans, she rang off. Only to accidentally answer Bianca's call.

"Hey," said Sutton, putting it on speaker so she could pace.

"Hey! So you're coming back?"

"I am," she said, ferreting around till she found a tissue box, and carefully wiping her nose. "Excited to be up close and personal once more."

"Are you?" Bianca asked. "Because you sound kind of floopy."

"Probably just the phone line," she lied. "How are the new songs coming along? Any crowd favourites rising to the top?"

There was a beat before Bianca said, "Sure! Plenty."

"She's lying!" Sutton heard Francie call out in the background.

"*Shush,*" Bianca hissed, the blur of her voice making Sutton picture her turning away from the phone. "This isn't about us—I think she's having an existential crisis over there."

"About time," Francie called out.

"Bianca?" Sutton called. "What's going on?" Doing some band manager magic would be the very best thing for her right now.

"So last night Francie tripped over a stray cord, not ours, fell and hurt her wrist."

"I'm fine!" Francie insisted.

"And yet we cancelled tonight so she can ice and elevate. Now Gustav is refusing to pay for Francie's hospital visit, even though the fault was theirs, refusing to pay us for our gigs to date, and threatening to sue over the lost earnings for any future dates we miss."

As Francie and Bianca argued, Sutton began making plans in her head. Using the band, and their worries, to push out all thoughts of Dante, and her parents, and leaving this sweet place behind. Who had time to think about one's future when one's present was a constant tightrope?

Sutton stopped rubbing at her temple. Opened her eyes. And repeated her thought out loud.

"Who had time to think about one's future when one's present was a constant tightrope?"

Before her trip she'd have gladly trotted that line out with pride. Now, sitting on a bedspread covered in cabbage roses, a Minotaur lamp looking solemnly back at her, the scent of a gorgeous giant lingering in the air...

Dante.

Just thinking his name made her heart press hard against her ribs. *Grow three sizes*, she thought, her father's words coming back to her.

She looked to the door. Pictured him standing there, hand in his hair. Doing as she asked and leaving. Not because he agreed, but because he'd want to make sure she was happy before looking after himself.

Dante, she thought, a sigh sticking in her throat as she tried to imagine a future in which she never saw him again.

Only it was impossible. No matter how hard she tried. Making her wonder why the hell she was trying so hard.

For him, a small voice in the back of her head reminded her. She was doing this for him—sending him away before she really hurt him.

What a fool, she thought. *What a reckless, misguided thing to do.*

Then she kicked the bed. Then kicked at it some more. Before letting out a great rage-filled roar.

"All better?" Bianca asked through the speaker on her phone.

Sutton flinched, having forgotten they were even there.

"No, actually," she said.

"Give it another go," Francie shouted back. "Let it all out!"

Let it all out.

Sutton took in a long slow breath, and on her next breath out did just that.

She let out the worry she'd end up like her dad. Let out the fear she might be more like her mum. Let out whatever remained of the ticking clock that had had such a hold over her life. Let out her need to be all things to all people so they'd like her, love her, and maybe, this time, never let her go.

And something inside her shifted. Something huge. As if she'd been looking at her life through a particular lens, and that lens had been whipped away.

"Bianca?"

"Yep."

"You know how I've always made it clear that if you ever felt as if you'd outgrown me, I would be happy to pass you on to a bigger agency. I take it back. If you try to leave me, I will follow."

"Hell yeah, you will!"

Sutton nodded, and began bouncing from foot to foot.

"In fact, I'm going to get the Sweety Pies back too."

"Hell yeah, you are!"

"And it's past time I hire an assistant. And maybe get a budgie. Or a goldfish. Whatever my neighbour will happily look after when I'm away."

"Your neighbour?"

"In the new flat I'm going to buy."

"Okay, you've lost me now."

Sutton fell back on the bed, arms out, total starfish. And she started to laugh. And laugh. And laugh.

"Definite existential crisis," Zhou muttered, before Sutton told them all she adored them, and would call again soon with news on how she planned to get them out of the Liefdescafé contract, but not before making the horrid manager pay through the nose.

Phone now silent, she glanced sideways, at her suitcase—half packed, for she'd done a half-assed job. As if the whole thing had been performative, only she'd honestly had no clue. Faking it, till she was certain leaving was the *only* choice.

Which she was—mostly. For both their sakes.

And yet, she let her next thoughts move inside her head with grace. Thought about planes and plans and amazing venues that would kill for a band like the Magnolia Blossoms to headline.

A few days later, as Dante stalked through the Vine kitchen—the staff scattering, aware that their temporary boss had been in a thunderous mood—he banged into Niccolo before he even saw him.

It took him a minute to recognise his cousin in his suit and tie, rather than the usual volunteer gear.

"Whoa," said his cousin on a laugh. "What's the rush, big guy?"

"No rush." Dante glared at Niccolo. "Some of us work around here."

"Some of us. But not you, right? Not anymore?"

He was right. Dante had "given his notice." Yet Nico's smile as Dante glared at him made Dante want to wrestle him to the ground as they had as kids.

"I get it," said Nico, slapping him on the arm. "My mother can drive the sanest person crazy. Piece of advice, try not walking around, all hunched and cantankerous, looking as if secretly imagining how you might burn the place down. You've done such a good job building the place up."

Dante, feeling the pinch in his shoulders, the

sneer on his lips, sucked in a breath and slowly rolled his shoulders, putting him an inch over his cousin's height. His cousin was right—he could feel as rotten as he liked, the staff and customers at the Vine did not need to bear the brunt of it.

His mood was not their fault. It was entirely his own. For he'd left, giving Sutton what she'd told him she wanted. He'd left, *knowing* she was dead wrong.

"Better," said Nico, grinning wider and whistling as he strode into the Vine proper, where he happily chatted up the bustling clientele.

Dante took a second to centre himself before he pushed through the swinging door. And what had started out as a quiet spot for stray tourists, and happy-hour locals, was now a thriving concern. Filled with ambient music, lit with a canopy of stars, left over from the singles night.

Something new was happening at the far end of the space, where they usually kept spare tables and chairs. Storage? Construction? Lots of wires and wood seemed to be involved? Something Chrissy and Kent had assured him they were on top of as it was no longer his concern.

After walking out of Sutton's bedroom, he'd driven straight to Vermillion Hill and told Zia Celia he was leaving. He offered three days to tie off loose ends. She'd not asked why, not asked how Sutton felt about that. She looked at him, and negotiated a week.

That date had passed two days earlier, and he was still hanging around. Because as far as he knew, Sutton was still in town. He did not know why—could only assume it had something to do with discharging the reason she'd come to Vermillion in the first place.

He'd not seen her, not once. Though he could feel her everywhere. Walking down Main Street, at the local grocer who stocked the raspberries she loved, at the vineyard, since he'd taken her on a tour of the entire place.

Yet knowing she was near meant he could not leave. Despite all that called him home, the invisible string tying him to her still pulled tight. Until he was sure she had left the country? Once he was certain she was safely back in the arms of those who loved her?

He knew he wasn't the only one. Despite her lauded independence, her support system was clearly wider and deeper than she realised.

Leaning against the edge of the bar, nearest the espresso machine, breathing in the scent of burned coffee beans, he knew what he'd just admitted to himself.

He loved her. Only it did not feel like news to him. It simply was. As if it had always been. Always would be. What a man did with that was beyond his expertise.

"Dante?"

Dante turned to find his aunt walking through the Vine's front door for the first time since he'd come to town. Her face lit up at the noise, the laughter, the electricity in the place.

"Zia Celia," he said, kissing her cheeks as she neared.

"Dante, this is more than I even expected. I can't believe the change that has come over this place. What's your secret?"

"Life," said Dante, "finding a way."

She must have heard some burr, some pain, in his words, for she turned to him, her expression concerned. "Life does that, you know. All you need to offer up is the smallest opening, and *la vita ritorna*."

Dante, well aware, having lived it over the past months, pressed a closed fist to his chest. To the place where his heart still beat stronger, even now, since letting Sutton Mayberry in.

Celia patted him on the cheek. "Now, might there be a table free, so an old lady can grab a light bite?"

Dante looked to Chrissy, who had been behind the bar, listening. She shrugged—no free tables.

"I believe there is one," said Dante, motioning with his head to the only table at which no customers sat.

Chrissy, nodding, hopped to it, grabbed a menu, and led Celia to the table by the last window. The one that still held a reserved sign. Even now.

Just as Dante's heart would forever be—reserved for the bolshie British brunette who had given it life again.

Sutton stood outside the Vine and Stein, looking up at the metal sign swinging from the horizontal pole over the door. The first time she'd seen it, her belly had been filled with anticipation. This time her emotions were far too fraught and too many to pin down.

Either way, something had sent her into *this* bar all those weeks before. The universe, fate, need for Wi-Fi—whatever it was, she'd had no idea that that moment was the true hinge on which her life would turn. For there was *before* she'd walked inside the Vine and Stein, and there was *after*.

She pushed open the door and was hit with a wall of white noise. Voices raised in conversation and laughter, from the group of people lined up before a lectern and the crowd filling the venue to near capacity. Kent, who was checking names against a booking calendar, looked up, saw her, and motioned for her to slip past.

Which she did, only to find the place looked like an absolute dream. The fairy lights in the ceiling had tripled since last she was there, the chandeliers had been dropped, hanging low over the crowd, and hidden fluoro rods she'd had Nico order and install added a pinkish dreamscape quality.

While at the far end of the space stood a purpose-built stage and small but effective light and sound rig. Dark purple velvet curtains swept from a centre point high above, curving to the edges of the stage, making it look fancier than it was.

It was just as she'd described it to Laila and Nico, Chrissy and Kent, who had all pitched in to make it happen, after she'd rung and explained her near-impossible idea. Which filled her with such poignancy, such honest joy, her heart hiccupped.

She apologised as she stood aside for staff she didn't recognise, moving through bussing glasses, then she slipped down the outer edge of the room, past her window, not looking to her table, in case someone else was using it.

All the while searching the crowd for a certain big, gruff Italian import. For if he wasn't there to see it, did it really exist?

Her spies had told her he was still around; still tying up loose ends, before he moved on. Some small part of her wondered if it was because he knew she'd not yet absconded, but that was the most wishful of thinking.

Either way, she wanted to give him this, this last hurrah to really set up the Vine for the future. To show Dante how much he meant to her, how much he meant to them all. Then maybe she could live with all the mistakes she'd made along the way.

And he could go home, to his beloved vineyard, and no longer feel beholden to anyone else's pull on his time. He could live his life, his passions, forevermore.

Dante, who'd been stuck at the vineyard the past couple of days—helping Celia train a handful of new sommelier recruits, something Nico could have done with his hands tied behind his back—went by the Vine to search for a "very important purse" Celia had left behind the other day.

While telling himself this was the very last thing he would do for the family. Underlined. Full stop. Then, once assured Sutton had left, he'd be on the next plane home.

Only the staff car park was full. Main Street the same. He had to park way down the road, and had built up a fair head of steam by the time he reached the Vine. Only to find the sounds coming from inside its walls none he'd heard before.

Pressing his way through the front door for the first time in days, he stopped, looked up at the sign, wondering if he'd walked into the wrong place. For it looked like a completely new place. Lights that he'd thought busted glowed gold and pink behind the mirrored wall behind the bar. The floor, having clearly had a polish, shone. And that was the least of it.

Pressing inside, he caught Kent's eye over the crowd.

"Mad, right?" Kent shouted from his spot behind the bar, slinging cocktails like he was born to it. "Can't believe she actually pulled this off."

She? Dante went to ask, only to realise he knew. There was only one person with the eye, the desire, and the tenacity to make such an event happen.

"Sutton." He realised he'd said it out loud, when Kent waggled a hand toward the back of the room.

The construction the others had waved off as a little upkeep turned out to be a stage. Speakers. Lights. Curtains. Then bodies walked out onto the stage, taking place behind drums, mike stands. Spotlights lit up and followed them, and the crowd pressed forward. The noise went through the roof.

"Dante! So glad you could make it!"

Dante turned to find Laila swishing past, cocktail in hand.

"Classic, cuz. Late to the party," said Nico, from his other side.

"Who is that?" Dante asked as the lead singer shouted something unintelligible into the mike before playing some raucous cacophony that sent the crowd wild.

"That would be the Magnolia Blossoms."

Dante looked to his left to find Sutton where Laila had been. Her hair tied back in a loose ribbon at her nape, small curls escaping at her cheeks. Looking mouthwatering in a black leather dress that dipped low in front, hugged her tight and stopped at her knees. She swayed in time with the music for a few beats, before her gaze lifted to his. *"Ciao."*

"Ciao," he managed, shaking his head. Mesmerised. Confused. Bursting with a life force that had flourished inside without him even knowing. "I thought… I thought you were leaving."

"Well," she said, leaning in closer so she didn't have to shout. Or so that she could lean in closer. Gods, how he hoped it was the latter.

"Turned out the Magnolia Blossoms were not being treated as they deserved by their last venue so I told them to come out here, and play a week of nights at this fabulous venue in the small winery town of Vermillion, South Australia." She shrugged. "I figured I'd better stay, at least until they arrived."

"How did you pull this off?" he asked.

"Told you once before, when I decide to do something, it gets done. Also, it turns out Kent's uncle works in immigration so put us onto the right people to get escalated visas. And if you give Laila a budget, not using her own money, she's a whiz with decor. Nico knows everyone, so staffing was a cinch."

Dante turned to find Nico now by the bar. He lifted a drink in salute, then flapped his hands, encouraging Dante to turn back around.

When he did, it was to find Sutton watching him. The band, the crowd, it all faded into insignificance as her eyes caught on his; hopeful, and wary, and bright. The crowd pressed in, knocking them toward one another. When their arms touched, she didn't pull away.

"Don't you want to know why?" she asked.

Dante was fairly sure he knew the why, but was happy to hear her say the words.

"It's time for you to go home, Dante. Stop looking after everyone here. That's what you want, isn't it?"

"*Si,*" he said. "At least that was what I wanted."

"Oh?" she said, her throat rising and falling.

He put a hand at her back when the crowd jostled them again. Ran his knuckles along her hips when he let her go. She rolled into his touch, heat sweeping into her eyes. And it was enough to help him say:

"I've been trying to pinpoint when that changed."

She swallowed, watching his mouth, waiting for his next words as if they were the air she needed to breathe.

"Was it the night you banged on the back door of the Vine, demanding to be let in? Or was it the day in the office, the delight on your face as you took in the picture of my family's vineyard? Perhaps it was that first morning, when despite how hard I tried to get you to leave, you refused me."

"Dante," she said, then licked her lips.

He lifted his hand to hold her chin, then dipped his mouth to hers. Tasting her glistening mouth.

"I couldn't go, not yet, knowing you were still here."

"I stayed," she said, "because you stayed."

Dante pulled her to his chest, the music reverberating through his shoes and into his bones. The beat of her heart against his drowning it out.

"Is it too late?" Her voice was light, but carrying to his ears anyway.

"Too late?" he asked. Knowing that for him, where she was concerned, time and place had no meaning.

"Is it too late to take back all the things I said the other day? I was overwhelmed, my head was a mess. And I think I took it out on you because you were the one thing I could trust."

She paused to take a breath, but Dante, hearing the words beneath her words, knew it was his turn to speak his truth.

"I love you, Sutton."

She breathed out hard. Her lashes fluttering wildly against her cheeks.

"I am in love with you," he said, leaning in to press his forehead to hers. "You took my heart the moment I laid eyes on you, and never gave it back. And if all this—" he motioned to the lights and the music and the crowd dancing around them "—means I have even the slightest hope that one day you might be able to return those feelings—"

Sutton threw herself into his arms, her head buried against his neck, words muffled. While he could have kept her there, his arms wrapped tight about her forever, he had a feeling those words might be worth hearing. He eased her back and said, "Could you say that again?"

"I love you so much, Dante. So much it scares me. In a good way. I thought it was a bad way. As in too much for me to handle. That if you didn't love me back, I might never recover. But then when you walked out my door, I realised that loving you *too much* is way better than any other life I might have. If I'm not too late, if I didn't screw everything up royally, I'm here now. Ready and willing. If you'll have me."

"I will have you, Sutton Mayberry, if you will have me. A humble, solitary, gruff, grape farmer."

She laughed, her head thrown back, and he pulled her closer.

"Are you sure you know what you're in for? Your life is dictated by sunshine, mine by moonlight. It's a mercurial existence."

"It's exciting," he amended, sliding a hand up her back, the other over the top curve of her backside.

"I'm impulsive."

"You're enthusiastic."

"I'm chaos."

"You're *vital*," he said, stressing the final word with so much passion, Sutton stopped coming up with reasons why they might not work. And hit on the one reason they would.

She gripped him tight, and lifted up onto her toes to whisper against his ear, "You are vital to me."

"Lucky then, for it seems we are vital to one another. From the moment I first saw your face, heard your voice, felt your stubbornness coming at me like a weapon, it was like the tolling of a bell. As if I'd been hit by... By..."

"Love lightning?" she asked, a small smile curving at the edge of her lovely mouth.

Dante took a moment, thought about the angle his life had taken. The colour, the light, the possibility that bled into every crack in his well-tended armour since coming to this place. And he said, "Love lightning."

Then noise rose as the crowd around them cheered. For a moment Dante thought it was for them, then he realised the band had stopped one song, pausing before the next.

She looked to the stage, to her band, and held up both arms and cheered. When her arms came back around his neck, Dante brushed his lips over her jaw, her ear, the edge of her mouth, and finally closed over hers.

More cheers went up around them, and most definitely *for* them.

When they pulled apart, she laughed, happy as he'd ever seen her, then turned so that she was watching her band, holding his arms around her.

Sutton, her head leaning on Dante's shoulder, said, "So I'd class tonight as yet another success."

"You would, would you?"

"We saved the bar. The girl got her guy." She tilted her head back and smiled. "If only I'd worn heels, so I could see better, then it would be perfect."

Dante sank down onto his knee, and pointed to his shoulders. "Get up," he said.

"What?" she called.

"Have you not been to a music festival before?"

Laughing, she took about half a second to agree, tucking her dress up to her thighs, she slung a leg over his shoulders, and whooped as he lifted her in the air.

She stayed up there for the whole song, singing at the top of her lungs, before she tapped out. Once on the floor, she thanked everyone around them. Explained they were her band. Promised them all a meet and greet with the band afterward.

After which Dante pulled her back in front of him, gathering her close, swaying with the crowd as the music, her band, cacophonous as they might be, became the soundtrack to what might be the best night of his life.

Best night so far, he thought, kissing the top of Sutton's head as she pressed back into him. *So far*.

EPILOGUE

Sutton sat at the long table on the east lawn of Villa Sorello, her laptop open, papers spread out, as she ticked off the final checklists for all that had to be in place for the big weekend ahead.

Francie came out carrying a plate of prawns. "No truly," she was saying to Celia, who carried a plate of eggplant parmigiana. "The sauce is a family recipe. We are famous for our seafood in Positano."

"Pfft," Celia scoffed. "No one is actually *from* Positano."

When Francie went to object, Sutton caught her eye, and shook her head. Francie, for once, in the face of Celia's Celia-ness, backed down.

A happy sigh on the tip of her tongue pretty much at all times these days, Sutton looked around, taking in the soft sunshine, the plates upon plates of wonderful food, the earthy scents making the place feel like some hazy dream.

But this was no dream. This was her life now.

Splitting her time between London—visiting her

dad as often as she could, when he was home—
and traveling with her bands. But most of her time,
more and more as the months went on, she spent
here, in this most beautiful of places, with the man
that she loved.

Bianca came bustling out of the side entrance,
carrying her famous *bitterballen*, Dutch meatballs.
Zhou had made cranachan, a creamy raspberry
dessert. And Dante's cook had put on the usual
antipasto and pastas, along with several bottles of
local wine, decanted and ready for the enjoying.

They'd all wanted to contribute, knowing how
busy Dante was, on the verge of launching his first
cellared release—a ten-year-old Sagrantino he'd
bottled the year he'd bought the vineyard. Sutton was busy too, as organiser of the Note di Vino
music festival, due to take place on the gently slop-
ing lawn to the south of the Sorello estate that weekend.

"I do believe that is everything," said Celia.

And Sutton quickly checked a couple of more
emails before closing her laptop.

"Was that from Nico?" Dante asked, as he appeared at Sutton's side.

"It was. He still thinks we should have called
the festival Grapestock."

Dante, grinning, passed her a bottle of lager,
chilled to the touch. He kissed the top of her head
as she took it, murmuring, "I must really love you
if I can handle watching you drink that swill."

"You love watching me do just about anything, I've found."

"True," he said, nipping at her neck, before he took the seat beside hers.

The Magnolia Blossoms, Crochet, and the Sweety Pies—still under new management, yet attending as headline guests—were all staying in the village, in preparation for the weekend. Her dad and Marjorie were coming the next day. Nico had stayed in Vermillion to "keep an eye on things," though Laila, also in Vermillion, running her beloved bookstore, kept messaging, saying she was certain Nico hadn't come as he was still pouting that his name wasn't chosen.

Once everyone was seated, food piling up onto plates, conversation flying, Dante's hand landed gently on Sutton's neck, his calloused fingers caressing her hair out of the way so he could touch her skin.

Her hand landed on his thigh, tracing circles that were just shy of risqué in such company.

Dante looked her way, leaned in for a kiss, mouthed, *"Ti amo,"* then drank his beloved wine.

Sutton listened for a tick, or a tock, and heard neither. Only the gentle hum of bees, the rustle of pencil pines, and the quiet, steady thud of her happy, happy heart.

* * * * *

If you enjoyed this story,
check out these other great reads
from Ally Blake

Always the Bridesmaid
Secretly Married to a Prince
Cinderella Assistant to Boss's Bride
Fake Engagement with the Billionaire

All available now!

Harlequin® Reader Service

Enjoyed your book?

Try the perfect subscription for Romance readers and get more great books like this delivered right to your door.

See why over 10+ million readers have tried Harlequin Reader Service.

Start with a Free Welcome Collection with free books and a gift—valued over $20.

Choose any series in print or ebook.
See website for details and order today: